LAW OF ATTRACTION

A FABLE

MR. MOON & FRIENDS'
SIMPLIFIED BLUEPRINT TO
HEALTH, WEALTH AND HAPPINESS

W. K. ATKINSON

LAW OF ATTRACTION
A FABLE

MR. MOON & FRIENDS' SIMPLIFIED BLUEPRINT TO HEALTH, WEALTH AND HAPPINESS

W.K. ATKINSON

http://LawOfAttractionToday.com

ISBN 978-1-9338-1756-9

Published by Profits Publishing
http://profitspublishing.com/

US Address
1300 Boblett Street, Unit A- 218
Blaine WA, 98230

Phone: 866-492-6623
Fax: 250-493-6600

Canadian Address
1265 Charter Hill Drive
Coquitlam, BC, V3E 1P1

Phone: 604-941-3041
Fax: 604-944-7993

Dedicated to the loving memory

of my sister,

Katherine Carlson

Table of Contents

CHAPTER 1

THE CAT AND THE TWO MICE

Once upon a time, in a land far away, there stood a castle in a clearing amid a magical, dense forest. The castle was filled with servants and masters whose flurry of activities penetrated the air with a myriad of diverse sounds. However, unbeknownst to these humans, sounds of a completely different nature would begin just before they arose from their sleep and continue long after they retired for the night.

"Arthur!" yelled Freddie the Mouse. "Where are you, Arthur?"

"I'm in bed, Freddie! I'm trying to sleep!" hollered his older cousin as he flipped over impatiently and pulled the covers over his perfectly round mouse ears. "It's well after your bedtime, for goodness sakes! Come to bed!"

Freddie stuck his head through the arched doorway and peered inside the immaculate mouse house. Peeping into the dim light, he appeared to wear a patch over one eye as half of his face was hidden behind a

CHAPTER 1: THE CAT AND THE TWO MICE

large, black blotch. The balance of his silky, white fur looked like it, too, was smattered with stains of black ink.

He and his cousin, Arthur, lived in the nicest mouse house in the county. Their domain, which was strategically situated in the main kitchen area of the castle, had been carefully constructed under the supervision of the head cook. The purpose of the mouse house was to accommodate two, hard working mice who could handle the extermination of bugs. As a reward to the mice for doing their job, the dwelling was suitably positioned in a corner where crumbs and drops and flakes would mysteriously end up directly in front of their door at least three times a day. On some mornings, Freddie and Arthur would wake up to bits of yarn, cotton balls, gumdrops and even pieces of Popsicle sticks. These items would greatly assist them in creating an environment that was both appealing to look at and comfortable to live in all year round.

Neither Freddie nor Arthur could recall how they ended up living in a castle. Perhaps they were born there. Perhaps they found the castle while looking for shelter in the dead of winter. Perhaps the humans who lived in the castle captured them for their own intents and purposes. In any case, their warm and cozy world made them happy and content. Life was good at the castle and the two mice were forever grateful for each other's company.

For as long as he could remember, Arthur looked after his younger cousin, Freddie. Being the older, more mature of the two, he took a pragmatic approach to most things, whereas Freddie was always a bit too carefree for his own good. But Arthur loved his little cousin and could not imagine living without him. Overall, they made excellent roommates who mixed just enough fun with just enough gravity to strike a good, healthy balance.

Freddie's eyes searched for Arthur in the dim lamplight of the mouse house.

CHAPTER 1: THE CAT AND THE TWO MICE

"Come here, Arthur," he beckoned his cousin in hushed tones. "Hurry! Poopsie's fast asleep!"

Arthur's nose quivered with anticipation at the mere thought of creeping up on Poopsie and watching him twitch and turn. He quickly gathered his plump, little body from his mouse bed, gave his toffee colored fur a quick lick, and in the blink of an eye followed Freddie into the living room where Poopsie slept on his back in front of the fireplace.

Unlike most domestic cats, Poopsie slept on a sheepskin rug that was purchased exclusively for him, and cut to exact measurements that would further facilitate his utmost comfort. An oak plaque hung on the wall above his bed with the message 'Do Not Disturb The Cat' painted meticulously on it in large, black letters. A nightlight glowed softly near his tail and would remain illuminated throughout the hours of darkness.

His sleeping attire usually consisted of a red and white striped flannel nightgown with matching nightshades. However, on this particular evening, and it being a bit warmer than usual in front of the fireplace, he chose to sleep in the nude with only his fur to keep the impending night chill away.

Sleeping was Poopsie's favorite occupation. After all, he did not have a designated job like Freddie and Arthur. Rather, he belonged to the highest-ranking master of the house. The master had found him three years ago, when Poopsie had been left for dead with all nine of his pure white siblings, in a box at the end of the castle driveway.

As he was the only kitten born with a distinctive black tail, the master elected to keep Poopsie as the castle pet, and quickly gave his nine siblings away to plain country folk. Since then he was treated as a royal member of the family and spoiled rotten. Sitting on a lap now and

CHAPTER 1: THE CAT AND THE TWO MICE

then, and listening to the boring stories of humans was all he had to do to earn his keep. He could roam whenever he wanted to roam, sleep whenever he wanted to sleep, and eat whenever he wanted to eat.

To draw attention to his stomach, which growled at least a dozen times a day, and sometimes at night, Poopsie would merely sit at attention and meow in order to stir up the servants. Within minutes, they would present him with his personalized bowl of albacore tuna and an accompanying bowl of distilled water. Every night before bedtime, the head cook would serve him a warm bowl of milk and one sardine. Canned cat food of any kind was prohibited in the castle.

No matter which way he looked at the situation, it was a fantastic arrangement and one that left him feeling pretty smug. In fact, he even rather enjoyed being dressed up by the servants, and took pride in the fact that he never wore the same ensemble two days in a row.

Now in deep repose, positioned flat on his back on the sheepskin bed, Poopsie snored through his mouth and whistled through his nose. His rosy, wet ribbon of a tongue protruded from his front teeth, as his eyeballs darted back and forth, and up and down like opaque marbles mounted on tiny springs. His poker-straight, back legs shot directly ahead, as his front legs rested like two dead fish on his well-fed belly. His puppet-like, front paws bounced, and jerked, and twitched, as his long, black tail clocked time like a metronome, sweeping the floor back and forth, back and forth, back and forth. All in all, he looked quite ridiculous.

"Look, Arthur. He's dreaming."

"I know," whispered Arthur as he crouched down near Poopsie's head. "He's dreaming about chasing us."

Freddie hunched his shoulders and revealed his toothy, impish mouse grin. "Maybe we should just suck him up with the vacuum cleaner."

CHAPTER 1: THE CAT AND THE TWO MICE

"He'd be too fat for that, Freddie. Look at him!"

They both stared and giggled at Poopsie's potbelly as it rose and fell with each breath.

Freddie clapped his hands with glee as he jumped up and down. "I know! I know! Let's tie him up and paint his fur pink!"

"Sshhh!" whispered Arthur, pushing a finger against his tiny mouse lips. "You'll wake him up! Come on, then. It's time to get you back into your bed before Poopsie gets up for his midnight snack."

Upon returning to their mouse domain, Freddie put his mouse pajamas on and climbed into his mouse bed. "Arthur? Will you please read me a story?"

"Not again, Freddie," Arthur wined. "You are such a juvenile. And you have terrible mouse breath. Go brush your teeth straight away."

"Okay. But if I do, will you please, please read me a story?" he begged.

Arthur let out a long sigh at this most predictable ritual. "Sure, I guess."

In just a few minutes, Freddie raced back to his bed, jumped in, and pulled the covers over his nose. "Will you read me a story about Mr. Moon?" His black eyes glistened with anticipation in the lamplight. "Oh, please?"

"Not Mr. Moon again, Freddie."

"Please?" he persisted.

So Arthur reached under his bed for his big, old storybook and flipped through the tattered pages. "Well, okay, let's see. Here's one:

CHAPTER 1: THE CAT AND THE TWO MICE

Once upon a time, very far away, there lived a moon. But he wasn't just an ordinary moon...he was a very special moon, indeed. Mr. Moon loved all creatures, big and small. When he was in his fullness, and the night was bright, all would be affected by his good nature. Some creatures would run around, eyes wild with laughter and delight. Others would simply sit and howl at the sky. Mr. Moon was the very most popular moon in the whole universe. All creation, from the biggest tree to the littlest spider, loved him with all their hearts. But Mr. Moon was also very mysterious. Sometimes his presence manifested in a huge, round splendor. Other times, only a fraction of his fullness could be seen. And once in a while, when he was the most mysterious and elusive, his presence could not be found at all, except for a lovely silver lining around a cloud. But Mr. Moon loved his creatures so much that he made certain that his light would always, always, always be available for all to see in the night."

Before Arthur could even finish the first page of the story, Freddie the Mouse was fast asleep. His little body quivered with excitement as he dreamed of playing tag with Poopsie, the cat.

Early the next morning, a big, wet nose appeared through the doorway of Freddie and Arthur's mouse dwelling.

"Anybody here?" Poopsie's whiskers twitched and his mouth watered. "I dare say, you both would make a yummy mouthful. What a simply *purrfect* little side dish for my boring tuna. But, alas, I just don't feel like exerting myself today," he sighed dramatically. "I didn't sleep well."

The mice sat up in their beds and quickly wiped the sleep from their eyes. "Leave us alone, Poopsie," said Arthur. "It's only six o'clock in the morning. Go away!"

"Oh, you pesky, little mouse heads." He wedged his pink nose inside the doorway. "Come out, will you?"

CHAPTER 1: THE CAT AND THE TWO MICE

"What's the matter, Poopsie?" snorted Arthur. "Too fat to come in?"

"Chubby, Chubby, Chubby!" screeched Freddie as he jumped up and down on his bed.

Poopsie removed his nose from the door with disdain and tried to collect himself with as much dignity as he could muster. "My name, thank you very much, is not Chubby," he said with a slight English accent. "My name is Poopscapaleon Appotamus and I would very much like to be treated with some semblance of respect, if you don't mind." He tried to extend his paw into the mouse domain, but lost his balance and fell over into an embarrassing heap. "To be honest, I don't even know why I bother with you two. You're just a stupid pair of mice."

"If we're so stupid, why haven't you been able to catch us?" giggled Freddie.

"Because, you obnoxious little rodent, I am far too busy doing other important things. I am not a mouser, you know. Catching silly mice is quite beneath me. I am very much capable of chasing larger prey."

Upon hearing this ridiculous comment, Arthur rolled his eyes knowing full well that Poopsie was too cowardly to sleep without a nightlight, let alone chase anything bigger than a chicken.

"Why don't you go chase Roger, then?" he asked sarcastically. "You could use a bit of exercise, don't you think?"

"Who on earth would care to catch a stupid dog, anyway?" replied Poopsie as he admired the configuration of his Monday outfit, a red and white flowered smoking jacket, and white, silk *cataloons*. His black-rimmed spectacles accessorized his ensemble perfectly. "Besides, he's just an ugly bulldog. And he smells."

CHAPTER 1: THE CAT AND THE TWO MICE

In his exuberance, Freddie skipped and hopped towards Poopsie and then screeched to a halt in front of his paws. "He doesn't smell, Poopsie. After all, the servants give him a bubble bath every day. And they put that really nice powder on him after his blow-dry. Roger smells really nice."

"Right," replied Poopsie with disgust. "Anyway, mouse heads," he continued as he adjusted his black spectacles, "enough small talk for now. According to my calculations, today is Monday. I am here to confirm that Merle the Squirrel will be delivering our nuts at six o'clock sharp this evening, as usual."

Arthur shrugged. "Haven't heard otherwise."

"Superb! I just love those delectable, little morsels. Let's just hope we get a full pail for a change, shall we? What an utterly useless, stupid squirrel."

On that note, Poopsie reached into the mouse hole within inches of Arthur's tail, fell over again and immediately lapsed into a lazy catnap.

CHAPTER 2

THE BULLDOG AND THE SQUIRREL

Freddie teetered on the top of his lookout point, the mailbox at the end of the castle driveway. His pink tail shivered in the cool, autumn air. "I can't see him. I can't see Merle the Squirrel!"

Roger Earl of Henry's short, sturdy legs carried his bulldog frame down the driveway with a unique, sideways shuffle that was characteristic of his noble breed. He wore a red and white checkered hat perched atop his massive head, which gave him a slight air of nonchalance, despite the look of disdain on his face created by his droopy jowls. Having a small brim in front, and a somewhat stiff peak at the back, the cap sat comfortably between his floppy ears and gave him a rather nice profile.

Beneath the surface, Roger carried a huge chip on his shoulder. Orphaned as a puppy, a shadow of sadness followed him everywhere he went. Having no idea how he ended up living in a castle, he relished the fact that he was cared for in a manner fit for royalty. He rather enjoyed his daily bubble baths, and all the fussing, and preening, and grooming bestowed upon him by the servants.

Unlike the mice, he did not have to work for the attention he got. No responsibilities were assigned to him other than barking once or twice when a stranger approached the castle. That was just for show, of course. Roger was not a brave dog. Never having to fend for himself rendered him helpless when it came to more daunting tasks. However, despite his insecurities and the fact that he had a bit of a speech impediment, he felt safe, comfortable and content in the castle.

Almost every night before he went to sleep, Roger thought about his family. He had no recollection of them whatsoever. He wondered about his parents and what they looked like. Where did they live? What kind of humans looked after them? Were they happy? Did they eat well? He wondered about how many brothers and sisters he had. Were they girls or were they boys? Did they like eating mushy liver kibbles like he did? Were they afraid of water like he was? Did they like to roll in the mud after a good summer thunderstorm?

Most of all, Roger wondered about his mother. Was she beautiful? Was her fur fawn and white like his? Were her eyes the color of dark chocolate? Was she accustomed to bubble baths? Did she like to be brushed? Were her nails perfectly manicured? Did she smell pretty?

Although he felt anger towards his mother for having abandoned him, Roger knew in his heart that no other bulldog would ever be able to take her place. Sometimes, really late at night, he would be overcome by a lovely scent drifting high in the air like a warm, summer breeze. The distant familiarity of this wafting smell would bring tears to his eyes. Was this the scent of his mother? Was she still alive? Was she nearby? Was she thinking of him? He hoped so, but he knew that his vivid imagination could just be playing tricks on him.

CHAPTER 2: THE BULLDOG AND THE SQUIRREL

Roger's wide, black nose glistened in the fading sunlight as he approached his friends. "Well, uh, where is he, anyway? Where's Merle the Squirrel?" he asked in his low, low voice. "It's already past dinnertime. What a lazy, uh, good for nothing, useless squirrel."

Poopsie huffed and puffed when he caught up to Roger. Always obsessed with appearing his best, he immediately sat down and washed his face and ears until they looked polished. "You got that right, Bubba. Meeeeooow," he said crankily. "I am so hungry. I say we all just hide until he gets here and then eat him up right away." He let out a great yawn and fell over on his side. "I hate that squirrel."

Arthur scampered to the top of Roger Earl of Henry's hat and perched himself high above everyone. "Eat Merle the Squirrel?" he asked with wide, blank eyes.

Poopsie sighed. "You got a problem with that, mouse brain? Maybe we should eat you and your toothy, little cousin instead," he replied as he felt his stomach growl.

"You couldn't catch us anyway, fat cat. Not in that ridiculous outfit," Arthur snorted.

Poopscapaleon Appotamus rose and dusted himself off. He never could quite understand all the ribbing about his clothes. He actually found it quite... irritating. One had to find one's own style, after all. He understood that his chosen ensemble gave him a bit of a conceited air. However, being snotty was his birthright. The rest of his brothers and sisters were just run-of-the-mill tabbies adopted by run-of-the-mill families. He, on the other hand, lived in a castle. At twenty-one pounds, half the size of Roger, he felt like a king and had every intention of acting like one.

Reaching out for Arthur with claws extended, Poopsie collapsed once again in the cool grass. "Isn't this just such a *purrfect* day?" He rolled onto his back and stretched. With emerald green eyes half closed, spectacles askew, pink nose glistening and face smug, he continued, "Hmmm…what should be on the menu today? Should it squirrel or should it be nuts?"

Merle the Squirrel merrily skipped along while singing a song, just because he was so happy to be a squirrel. As he got closer and closer to the castle, he started to feel a bit queasy in his stomach. Looking into his pail, he counted only fourteen nuts. How was he going to explain this again to Poopscapaleon Appotamus, or Roger Earl of Henry, or Freddie and Arthur?

He stopped and put his little squirrel pail down. "Well," he said out loud in his childlike, sweet voice, "maybe I could say that half the nuts fell out while I was skipping along. Or maybe I could say that my pail had a hole in it. That sounds pretty good. Or maybe I could say that I could only find fourteen nuts today, or that half the nuts were stolen. Oh, my! Oh, my! What should I do? What should I do?"

Merle the Squirrel had been gathering nuts during the autumn season for the past two years, ever since he was old enough and strong enough to carry his little pail. The juicy filberts would fall from the trees of the nut farm near the castle where he would husk and collect them. Every Monday at six o'clock, he would deliver them to his designated drop-off point at the end of the castle driveway. Merle would never eat with his friends, but he would always observe them from a distance until the last nut was gone. He particularly liked to watch Roger smacking his big lips and spraying everyone with spit after his feast.

CHAPTER 2: THE BULLDOG AND THE SQUIRREL

Merle did not share the luxury of living in a castle, nor did servants feed him in the wintertime when snow covered the ground. So, unbeknownst to his friends, he would bury and stockpile enough nuts to help him survive the cold winters. This secret cache of nuts would also enable him to continue treating his friends. He knew they didn't need the filberts, but without this means of contact, the long days of winter would be much too lonely for him.

He really loved his friends. His parents had died only six months after he was born at the hands of a hungry raccoon, so Merle wandered the forest alone until he accidentally found the castle and met Roger, Poopsie, Arthur and Freddie.Oh, he knew they didn't particularly like him very much. After all, he was dirty, homeless and probably smelled bad, but they were the only friends he had and he fully intended to keep them.

Today, as usual, Merle the Squirrel went out looking for nuts. As it was the last Monday of the fall season, and the ground was already covered with frost, he was only able to find twenty-eight nuts. After burying half of them in the mud, his little pail felt lighter than usual.

"That only leaves three for each of my friends and two for me," he thought out loud as he skipped along swinging his pail back and forth.

Suddenly feeling vulnerable, he stopped and looked around. Surrounded by the dense forest and the dangers lurking within it, he bit his tiny squirrel claws and deliberated on what to do next. "I think I'm going to climb up the tallest tree I can find," he said. "That way, I will have more time to think."

In the blink of an eye he was gone, with only his graceful, long tail following behind him.

CHAPTER 2: THE BULLDOG AND THE SQUIRREL

With much strength and agility he ran up a big, old oak tree. Sitting on the highest branch, he felt somewhat safe. From his vantage point, he could observe all that occurred below him.

Merle recounted his nuts. Somehow, he had lost two nuts during his climb up the tree. He had only twelve left. "Oh my, oh my," he fretted. "I'm so hungry. And it's getting so dark. What am I going to do? What am I going to do?" he said, staring into his little squirrel pail.

Without another thought, he dipped his tiny hand into the pail and popped a nut into his mouth. Then he had another. Now he had ten nuts left out of the twenty-eight he had started with. Ten nuts would only give each of them two for dinner.

"Oh my, oh my," he repeated woefully through sleepy eyes.

Mr. Moon was just beginning to show his full face. Merle the Squirrel felt tired after his day of collecting nuts, and as hard as he tried to stay awake, finally curled up into a little ball and fell asleep, all alone in that big, old oak tree.

"Where the heck is Merle the Squirrel?" hissed Poopscapaleon Appotamus. "He knows dinnertime is at six o'clock sharp!"

Roger shifted back and forth. "It's kind of getting dark now. That stupid, uh, squirrel probably got lost."

"He's not that bright," added Arthur as he hugged Freddie for warmth. "Maybe something awful happened to him."

CHAPTER 2: THE BULLDOG AND THE SQUIRREL

"Oh, for Petie's sakes," replied Poopsie. "Who really cares? He's just a useless squirrel, anyway. All I want to do is eat him up. He can't even collect a full pail of nuts."

Roger Earl of Henry let out a hungry growl. "Maybe Merle the Squirrel is really in trouble. Maybe we should go out, uh, looking for him."

Poopsie adjusted his black spectacles. "Come on, you guys. I say we just call it a night. Who would ever miss that squirrel anyway? He's a nuisance. He's annoying. And he smells. Come on, let's go home."

"All right, that's enough," grumbled Roger in his low, low voice as he straightened his red and white checkered hat. "We're just wasting time talking about this. I'm hungry and I want my nuts. So, uh, what do you say we just go out and look for that stupid squirrel?"

They stood in silence for a minute. Poopsie finally nodded. "Okay, all right. But we've never been out this late before and, quite frankly, I don't like the thought of it. It'll be dark before too long and none of us has ever ventured into the forest. I'm tired, I'm hungry and I'm getting cold, so let's get this over with as fast as we can, shall we? And let me tell you, if anything happens to me, it'll be that annoying squirrel's fault."

And thus, on command from Roger Earl of Henry, the foursome rounded up and set out into the deep, dark forest to find Merle the Squirrel, and more importantly, his pail of nuts.

CHAPTER 3

MR. MOON

Merle the Squirrel woke up with a start. He quickly stood up on his hind legs and curled his little squirrel hands flat against his chest. "Hello? Is somebody there?" he asked in a trembling voice. "Hello?"

"Why, hello, Merle the Squirrel."

Merle gasped in fright and then let out a happy sigh. "Mr. Moon! How did you know I was here?" he asked as he wiped the sleep from his eyes.

Mr. Moon's full, white splendor hung in the sky like a giant pie plate. "Your beautiful, gray tail was silhouetted against my light," he answered in a soothing, fatherly voice. "It looked so long and silky that I had to investigate further. I thought you might be a wild beast of the forest!"

"Oh, thank you so much, Mr. Moon. But as you can see, I am just an ordinary squirrel." A single teardrop fell from his eye and he quickly brushed it away with his bushy tail.

CHAPTER 3: MR. MOON

"What makes you so sad, Merle?" asked Mr. Moon.

"I'm all alone and I miss my friends," he answered in his teeny voice. "I think I'm a little bit scared, too."

"You need not be scared, Merle the Squirrel. As long as I am here, you will never be alone or in danger. What are you doing in such a tall tree at this hour?"

Peering into his pail, he answered tearfully, "These nuts are for my friends. I was supposed to deliver them by six o'clock, but I lost my nerve."

"Why is that?"

Merle stood on his hind legs again and revealed his muddy, white tummy. He looked at Mr. Moon earnestly through his big, round eyes. "They always expect a full pail of nuts, but I only ended up with fourteen today. I didn't want them to get mad at me again, so I decided to climb the tallest tree in the forest and think about what I should do. While I was climbing up the tree, I lost two nuts along the way. Then I ate two because I was so hungry." He added sadly, "I only have ten nuts left."

Mr. Moon listened patiently and answered calmly, "I see."

Merle dipped his dirty, teeny hand into the pail and then, with an outstretched arm, offered two nuts to Mr. Moon. "If you're hungry, sir, you can have my share if you like."

"No, thank you, little one," he said tenderly. "But I won't forget your generosity. Right now I have something very important I have to do. But since I can be in many places at once, why don't you rest for a while in my light where you'll be safe? Sweet dreams, Merle the Squirrel."

CHAPTER 3: MR. MOON

As Poopsie, Roger, Freddie and Arthur inched their way through the foreboding forest looking for Merle the Squirrel and their share of nuts, Mr. Moon peered down at them.

"Look, Arthur!" shouted Freddie. "There's Mr. Moon!"

Poopsie straightened his jacket and quickly licked his fur. "Hello, Mr. Moon," he greeted. "We are looking for Merle the Squirrel. Have you seen him?"

"Indeed," replied Mr. Moon in a most serious tone.

"Well, where is he, Mr. Moon? He's, uh, got our nuts and I'm getting really hungry," growled Roger.

Mr. Moon's eyebrows came together in a scowl and his light dimmed. "So a big, strong bulldog like you expects to get food from a defenseless, little squirrel, Roger Earl of Henry? A bulldog who lives in a castle?"

Roger's big, old tongue hung out the side of his mouth like a wet dishrag as he contemplated the question.

Mr. Moon continued in a booming tone, "And from a defenseless, little squirrel that you call stupid and useless?"

His eyes then riveted on Poopsie. "What about you, Poopscapaleon Appotamus? Not only do you call this squirrel stupid and useless, but you also threaten to eat him. Is that correct?"

Feeling embarrassed and ashamed, Poopsie hung his head and answered quietly, "Yes."

CHAPTER 3: MR. MOON

"Freddie? Arthur? Do you have anything to say?"

Too afraid to speak, the two mice quickly hid under Roger's hat.

Mr. Moon's light became brighter and his eyes grew darker. "All of you should be ashamed of yourselves! What is the meaning of this?"

"But we are looking for him, Mr. Moon. That should say something, shouldn't it?" said Poopsie. "I mean, we could have just left him out in the cold," he added in his bravest voice.

"Poopscapaleon Appotamus! If it were up to you, you certainly would have left him out in the cold. The only interest you have of Merle the Squirrel is his cache of nuts!"

Poopsie looked up with one eye. "How did you know that, sir?"

"I know everything," answered Mr. Moon, "down to the whereabouts of the smallest sparrow in the forest. Any time you pass judgment on that harmless, sweet, defenseless, little squirrel, you pass judgment on me. So would you like to look me square in the eyes right now and call me 'stupid' or 'annoying' or 'useless'? Would you like to eat me, too?"

Poopsie sunk as low as he could go. "No, sir. But I didn't really mean those things in the first place."

"He is far too innocent to know the difference. And as much as you continue to take advantage of him and to hurt his feelings, he still goes out faithfully every Monday of the fall season to gather nuts for you. He still considers all of you his friends." Glaring at the foursome, he added gravely, "This situation is totally unacceptable to me."

Roger Earl of Henry stepped forward. "Well, uh, I cannot help the

CHAPTER 3: MR. MOON

way I am. I'm an orphan, after all, and I carry that burden with me everywhere I go."

"Roger Earl of Henry, whatever your past circumstances may have been, I hold you fully responsible for all your actions in the present. You are not a child anymore. You are an adult who can make responsible decisions. You go now, all of you, and rescue Merle the Squirrel."

Poopsie inched forward. "But we have never been in the forest, sir. And it is getting very cold. And there must be dangers lurking in every corner."

"Indeed. Now you must experience the same conditions as Merle the Squirrel who sleeps alone and in fear every night."

Poopsie bowed his head. "Yes, sir."

Not one of the four had anything further to add. With no further hesitation, they set out into the darkening forest guided only by the light of Mr. Moon. Not a word was spoken amongst them. Not a sigh was heard. Not a sneeze. Not a cough. They were all lost in their own thoughts of how wretched they felt to have disappointed Mr. Moon.

Thirty minutes passed and the air cooled. Poopsie buttoned his smoking jacket and shoved his hands into his pockets. The two mice scampered up Roger's back and took shelter under his red and white checkered hat.

Then suddenly, and for no apparent reason, their guiding light vanished and the night became as black as soot.

Freddie, who was terribly afraid of the dark, freaked out. "Mr. Moon's light went out! Mr. Moon's light went out!" he shrieked in terror as he clutched Arthur.

CHAPTER 3: MR. MOON

Poopsie's eyes shone like jewels in the darkness. "Don't get your knickers in a knot, mouse brain. I can see in the dark. I'm a cat, after all." Adjusting his spectacles, he looked around and around and around, but to his utter horror, he saw absolutely nothing. "Mary, Mother of Jesus!" he exclaimed, suddenly feeling faint. "I cannot see a thing!"

Roger's presence was only detected by his overwhelming bulldog odor and the sound of his big, old heart thumping in his chest. "Uh, okay, let's pull ourselves together and just ask Mr. Moon why he turned his light off."

He looked up into the black sky. "Uh, Mr. Moon? Mr. Moon? It's Roger Earl of Henry here. We noticed that you, uh, turned your light off. Can you turn it back on, please, because we cannot see a thing? The mice are freaking out and Poopsie has fainted from fright."

A silence hung in the air like a heavy mist.

"Uh, I said, Mr. Moon? Are you there? I say, are you there, Mr. Moon?" Roger raised his low, low voice.

Freddie and Arthur wailed at the top of their little mouse lungs, "We're blind! We're blind!"

In the commotion, Poopsie picked himself up and brushed himself off in total embarrassment as though everyone could plainly see him. Feeling quite woozy, he sat down again and shielded his ears from the piercing screams of the mice.

Like a blast of thunder, Mr. Moon's disembodied voice boomed, "Quiet! I don't want to hear another word from any of you. No screaming. No crying. No talking. Now, listen, all of you! I have not turned my light off. The truth of the matter is that you are too overwrought with guilt

CHAPTER 3: MR. MOON

and shame to see it. You must make amends with Merle the Squirrel or you will never see in the dark again."

Trembling in the dark, cold night and more afraid than they had ever been before, the foursome sounded a huge gasp as they huddled together.

"But it's so dark, for Petie's sakes! What if we get lost?" asked Poopsie, who was getting more and more petrified by the minute.

"Poopscapaleon Appotamus, it is in adversity that your biggest accomplishments will come," answered Mr. Moon. "And remember this," he added, "you will always be as big as your faith or as small as your ego. The choice will be yours. Go now, all of you, and find Merle the Squirrel."

So once again, Roger, Poopsie, Freddie and Arthur slowly, and very reluctantly, turned to face the ominous forest.

Mr. Moon, who could no longer be seen, hung close in the sky and smiled.

CHAPTER 4

MR. MOON'S WISDOM

"One, two, three, four, five, six, seven, eight, nine, ten." Merle counted the nuts over and over again as he lined them up on the tree branch and then carefully put each one back into his pail.

Mr. Moon peeked down at Merle. "Everything okay, little one?"

"Oh, hello, Mr. Moon! You're back!"

"What are you doing? I thought you would be sleeping."

"Oh, I'm just counting my nuts. Now I wish I hadn't buried half of them in the mud."

"The nuts you buried have to sustain you throughout the entire winter season. But your friends are well fed in the castle during the winter. Why do you keep bringing them filberts? You need only to bury enough for yourself."

CHAPTER 4: MR. MOON'S WISDOM

"Oh, I just wouldn't feel right if I didn't share, Mr. Moon. Besides, if I didn't deliver the nuts to them, they wouldn't want to see me at all."

"I see."

"But I am so hungry now. I really wish I could have just one more. Should I, Mr. Moon?" He rubbed his shrunken belly as another teardrop rolled down his cheek.

"That is a difficult question to answer, Merle the Squirrel. Perhaps I will tell you that to have exactly what you want all the time is called 'richness', but to be able to do without is called 'power'. And if you could see yourself the way I see you, you would know, beyond any doubt, that you are a very powerful, little squirrel."

"Me?" he asked incredulously as he pointed to the center of his chest.

"Indeed. So whenever you are in doubt about anything at all, just remember that it is much better for you to make a decision based on what is right or wrong for everyone, rather than what is good or bad for Merle the Squirrel. The right decisions become wonderful investments and will serve you well in the future."

"What are investments, Mr. Moon?"

"You shall see in time. For now, why don't you put your pail away and try to get a little sleep."

Mr. Moon slid down the sky to a place not far from that big, old tree. The warmth from his light covered Merle the Squirrel like a cozy blanket.

But Merle tossed and turned for the longest time. All he could think of were his friends and how much he missed them. He couldn't wait to see them again. Oh, he knew they would chastise him for not bringing a full

CHAPTER 4: MR. MOON'S WISDOM

pail of nuts and he knew they would belittle him for being late. He was just an ordinary squirrel, after all, not a royal member of a castle. Merle couldn't remember the last time he bathed, let alone ate a full meal or slept under shelter. He felt lucky they would speak to him at all.

"Still can't sleep, little one?" Mr. Moon whispered.

He rubbed his dirty tummy and felt hungrier than he had ever been in his entire life. "I'm just not that tired, sir."

"If you can't sleep, we can talk for a while."

Merle scampered to the very end of the tree branch and perched as close to Mr. Moon as possible. "What are we going to talk about?" he asked excitedly.

"Anything you like, Merle. Or we could play a game, if you prefer."

"Really? Will you really play a game with me?"

"Yes, of course! Why don't we play *I Spy With My Little Eye*? Do you like that game?"

Merle's little, black nose quivered with anticipation. "It's my favorite! I play it with myself all the time! You first!"

"Okay, then. Let's see. Hmmm…I spy with my little eye…something that is…behind you."

Merle turned around so quickly that he almost lost his balance. "Could it be my tail?"

Mr. Moon laughed heartily. "That was a very good guess, little one. No, it's not your tail. Guess again."

CHAPTER 4: MR. MOON'S WISDOM

"Okay. Is it this tree?"

"No, but you are getting warmer. Try one more time."

Merle the Squirrel's eyes became as big as saucers as he thought and thought and thought. "Can you please give me another clue, Mr. Moon?"

"I think that would be fair. I spy with my little eye…something that is IN the tree."

Merle jumped up and down with joy. "That has to be me! That has to be me!"

"You are really close now, little one. Look behind you!"

Merle quickly turned around and there, to his utmost surprise, wedged between the trunk of the big oak tree and the tree branch, was the biggest, shiniest pail of nuts he had ever seen in his life.

"WOW! WOW! WOW! Look! It's a giant pail of nuts, Mr. Moon! Now I'll have lots to share with my friends!"

"Can I let you in on a little secret, Merle? Even if you eat half the nuts in this pail, you will still have enough to fill your other one."

"You mean, I can eat some? Right now?"

Mr. Moon's eyes crinkled at their corners. "Yes, my precious one, you can eat them right now."

"But are they really mine, Mr. Moon? Are they?"

"Indeed. You attracted them to yourself. They are all yours."

CHAPTER 4: MR. MOON'S WISDOM

Merle's eyes looked like two black pies on his little face. "How did I do that?"

"Everything you do out of genuine love will expand in your life. The forest will give you many times over what you give away. That is the law. Sometimes you will receive surprises from a source you least expect, and at a time you least expect. You see, giving something away means you already have an abundance of it. Therein lies the secret and the magic of the forest."

Merle's forehead furrowed as he thought very hard. "So did the pail of nuts come from you?"

Mr. Moon laughed and laughed. "Everything comes from me, little one. But I didn't put them there. You did!"

"Me?"

"Yes, you! You hid the pail of nuts in this tree a very long time ago when the filbert season flourished and your pail overflowed. You wanted to save them for your friends, in case you ran out someday. That decision, which was made out of love, sent out a message to the forest that was answered in a very good way and in its perfect timing. You see, the fact that you picked this tree to sit on this evening was certainly no coincidence."

Merle stood on his hind legs and stared at Mr. Moon intently while he attempted to absorb the fullness of his words.

"Merle, whenever you make 'right decisions' you must always trust a good outcome because 'right decisions' are based on love and put you in alignment with the forest's unlimited abundance and power. And these decisions are like boomerangs, which will return much goodness to you in time.

CHAPTER 4: MR. MOON'S WISDOM

This wonderful, magnificent forest is a place where you can paint your own canvas of life in any way you like, a place where you become a creator through your thoughts, your feelings and your imagination, a place where the outer forest will always mirror the inner you.

The forest is a friendly place, Merle the Squirrel. Everything that happens in it is for your highest good. You may never understand all its secrets, but it will always be on your side."

"I don't know if I completely understand what you are saying, Mr. Moon," said Merle in his sweet voice.

"That's all right, little one. Suffice it to say, be happy no matter what your circumstances are, keep good things in your heart and in your mind at all times, and embrace the joy that comes from loving and serving others. If you do these three things and nothing more, you will experience magic in your life.

And most importantly, Merle the Squirrel, always remember that you are a very powerful squirrel. I am always inside of you. I am with you everywhere you go."

As they shuffled inch-by-inch, step-by-step, through the scary forest in the dead of the night, Roger and Poopsie looked quite ridiculous with their arms wrapped around each other. Freddie and Arthur added a further comic dimension to the foursome by bobbing up and down underneath Roger's red and white checkered hat.

"What are we going to do?" asked Roger. "We, uh, have no idea where we are going."

CHAPTER 4: MR. MOON'S WISDOM

"I'll tell you one thing," said Poopsie. "Without Mr. Moon's light, we'll never find Merle the Squirrel."

"But, uh, if we don't find Merle the Squirrel and apologize, we're never going to see in the dark again."

Poopsie stopped. "Look, Roger, I say we stay where we are. If we can't see where we're going, we could hurt ourselves. Maybe we should sleep for a while and then continue on tomorrow."

Arthur peeked from under Roger's hat. "Maybe we should try calling Mr. Moon again."

"Do you see Mr. Moon, sawdust head? He's gone. The best thing we can do is stay here until Mr. Sun's shift starts in the morning."

"But we can't sleep standing up," said Roger. "How are we going to sleep? It's too cold to sleep on the ground."

Even though he could not see a thing, Poopsie straightened his black spectacles. "Good point, Roger. I have given it some thought and I believe we will have to sleep on my jacket."

So he removed his favorite red and white flowered smoking jacket and carefully placed it on the damp ground. "Lie down on my jacket, Roger, and the three of us will sleep on top of your stomach."

"Like, uh, I'm going to be your mattress for the night?"

"Look, dog breath, I don't exactly relish the idea of sleeping on your smelly, old belly either. Do you have a better idea? Besides, the mouse heads will freeze to death if we don't get them warm in a hurry. Then what would Mr. Moon say?"

"Well, uh, if you put it that way, I guess it will be okay."

CHAPTER 4: MR. MOON'S WISDOM

So Roger Earl of Henry carefully lowered his rotund body onto Poopscapaleon's jacket. Rolling over on his back, his stubby legs pointed straight in the air, except for his limp paws. "Oh, man. Uh, this is so uncomfortable."

"It's no sheepskin bed, flea bag, but it will have to do for the night."

So Poopsie, Arthur and Freddie curled up into their respective little balls and buried their heads in Roger's soft, belly fur. It took no time at all for the foursome to fall asleep.

CHAPTER 5

EDDIE THE EAGLE

Roger Earl of Henry seldom went to bed on an empty stomach, but when he did, he dreamed. When he dreamed, he snored. Not only did he snore, he also twitched. On this particular evening, Roger snored and twitched, snored and twitched, snored and twitched. As he shook and shimmied and jerked, his inhalations could suck up the largest bug in the forest and his exhalations would make his jowls flutter and drool. His dreamland consisted of heaping bowls of liver kibbles and bits.

From his vantage point atop a nearby tree, Eddie the Eagle watched the intriguing scenario unfold below him.

"Wow," he said matter-of-factly. "Isn't that a sight for sore eyes? Hey, Frank! Come take a look at this, will you?"

Frank joined his friend, Eddie, on the tree branch and zoomed in with his binocular vision for a closer look. At first, he just stared in total disbelief. Then he shook his head a few times, blinked a few times, and stretched his long neck out as far as he could to look again.

CHAPTER 5: EDDIE THE EAGLE

"So what do you make of it?" asked Eddie the Eagle.

"Looks like Roger Earl of Henry is having a heart attack. Wait... wait just a minute! What's that on his stomach?"

Sitting side by side, they both craned their necks out even further.

"Oh, it can't be," said Eddie.

But it was, indeed. Even though Roger sputtered and spit and drooled and twitched, Poopsie, Arthur and Freddie were nestled as snug as bugs on his big, warm belly, totally oblivious to the scene they were creating.

"Would you look at that?" said Eddie to himself.

"What do you think is going on?" asked Frank. "Do you think they're in trouble? Why are they out here in the middle of the night, anyway?"

"Don't know, Frank. I suppose there's only one way to find out."

With his two-meter wingspan spread wide and mighty, Eddie silently glided to the ground below. In the blink of an eye, he snatched Freddie the Mouse from his sleep and then took flight into the night.

"Help! Help! Somebody help me!" screamed Freddie in an ear-piercing voice.

Waking up from a deep sleep, Poopsie lifted his heavy head from Roger's warm belly and tried to focus, but the night was as black as coal.

CHAPTER 5: EDDIE THE EAGLE

Arthur jumped to attention and looked around for his cousin, but the darkness hung heavily around him.

Totally disoriented, Roger Earl of Henry wiped the drool from his chin and grumbled, "Uh, what's happening? What's happening?"

"Help me! Pleeeeeease! Somebody, help me!" squealed Freddie.

"Quit your hollering, you wretched little mouse," yelled Poopsie, as he adjusted his black spectacles. "Come back down here right away, wherever you are!"

But as soon as the threesome became fully awake, they could barely hear Freddie's little voice. It seemed to oddly fade into a muffled whimper.

"I'm up here!" he called out desperately.

"Well, dog gone it," said Roger as he looked up. "Uh, will someone tell me what the heck's going on?"

"I'm up here!" The squeaky voice seemed to hang far above them.

"Well, dog gone it, anyway," said Roger again. "Will somebody, uh, turn the lights on so I can see what's going on?"

Arthur squinted, rubbed his eyes, stood on his tiptoes and turned his head from side to side. Then, with the loudest cry possible from a teeny, tiny mouse, he screamed, "Freddie! Where are you? I can't see you!"

"Shut up, mouse brain!" shouted Poopsie in the commotion. "We can't see in the dark, remember? It's all that stupid squirrel's fault."

Amid the calamity, Freddie's voice drifted far, far away. "Help me! Help me!"

CHAPTER 5: EDDIE THE EAGLE

"Well, where are you, for Petie's sakes?" Poopsie looked up in the direction of the small, fading plea for help.

Suddenly, they heard a flutter, then a loud swoosh and Freddie's voice could be heard no more.

"Let me go!" Freddie tried to wiggle his little body free from the powerful talon. But Eddie ignored Freddie's appeal and flew high above the forest.

"Let me go, I said," cried Freddie again.

Eddie landed softly on top of a telephone pole. "Try to relax, Freddie. I'm not going to hurt you," he responded in a gentle, but authoritative voice.

"Is that you, Eddie the Eagle?"

"Yes, Freddie, it's me. Can't you see me? Is something wrong with your eyes?"

Freddie's small whimper quickly developed into uncontrollable sobbing. Huge tears fell on his chubby mouse cheeks.

Eddie tried to comfort the little mouse by tickling him on the back of his neck with his massive beak. "Don't cry, Freddie, I'm not going to hurt you. But you know this forest is my territory. I am the watchman. So why don't we start from the beginning. Is something wrong with your eyes?"

Sniffling and snorting, he wiped his teary eyes with his tiny mouse hands. "We can't see anything, Eddie."

CHAPTER 5: EDDIE THE EAGLE

"What do you mean?"

"Well," he sniffled and snorted some more, "Mr. Moon said we can't see his light anymore because of our guilt and shame over being so mean to Merle the Squirrel. We called him names and made fun of him."

"I see. So why are the four of you sleeping out here in the forest?"

"Because Mr. Moon said we had to find Merle the Squirrel and apologize. But we couldn't see where we were going, so Poopsie said we should try to get some sleep until Mr. Sun's shift started in the morning. He put his coat down for Roger to lie on and we all jumped on his belly and went to sleep. It was the only warm place in the forest. Oh, Eddie, I'm so upset! What if something terrible happened to Merle the Squirrel? What will he do in the forest all by himself? It's so cold out here. I had no idea. None of us did. Maybe he's lost right now. Or maybe a hungry raccoon ate him up. And it's all because of those stupid nuts. I just feel so awful now, Eddie. Merle the Squirrel never complained even though none of us ever helped him out. All we did was call him bad names and then take our share of nuts from him." Freddie began to cry again. "I miss him, I really do."

Eddie the Eagle looked at Freddie intensely. "Do you understand how powerful words are and how destructive they can be?" he whispered.

Freddie lowered his head. "Yes, sir."

"Are you aware that bullying Merle the Squirrel was the wrong thing to do?"

"Yes, sir. But I never meant those things I said. None of us really did."

"Do you think Merle the Squirrel knows the difference between what you mean and what you don't?"

CHAPTER 5: EDDIE THE EAGLE

"No, sir." Freddie felt ashamed as his tears flowed again. "If only I could take it back, Eddie. Maybe I will never have the chance. Maybe it's too late."

"If you want to take it back, Freddie, I suppose there is only one thing to do. We'd better find Merle the Squirrel."

"Really?" shrieked Freddie the Mouse. "Do you really mean it?"

"Hey, Frank," he called out to his friend. "Man the fort, will you? Freddie and I have some business to attend to."

Without a sound, Frank swooped down to a clearing near Poopsie, Arthur and Roger, folded his majestic wings and stood watch as Eddie the Eagle and his charge flew high into the night sky.

Poopsie, Roger and Arthur huddled together for warmth.

"Uh, now I'm starting to feel really hungry," said Roger in his low, low voice.

"Would you quit thinking about your stomach for a change, dog breath?" said Poopsie as he shivered in the cold. "Can't you see the seriousness of our situation?"

"Well, I haven't eaten anything for a long time now, you know. And I'm a big dog."

"You're a fat dog and you can stand to lose a few, believe me."

CHAPTER 5: EDDIE THE EAGLE

"But I have to eat or I won't have the strength to find Merle the Squirrel."

"Guess what, pea brain? It's not all about you. It's not all about your stomach," hissed Poopsie. "We're all hungry. We're all tired. And for the moment, we're all blind as bats and alone in the forest. Survival is what it's all about, Roger, not your big, fat stomach. So shut up."

Arthur peered out from beneath Roger's hat. "Come on, Poopsie. Being mean won't get us anywhere. That's why we're in this mess in the first place. We have more important things to think about besides quarrelling amongst ourselves. We have to find Merle the Squirrel and Freddie."

"How to you propose we do that, mouse head? We can't see any further than our noses," scorned Poopsie who was clearly getting more anxious by the minute. His cozy bed and comforting nightlight were only a distant memory now as the menacing hours of darkness began to take hold in the damp, chilly forest.

"Maybe we should ask Mr. Sun what to do," suggested Arthur.

Poopsie nodded. "Good idea. Maybe Mr. Sun will help us out. We'll ask him how we can find Merle the Squirrel, and then we will be able to see in the dark. And we'll ask him to help us find Freddie, too. Let's conserve our energy for now and go back to sleep."

So Poopsie took his soiled and tattered jacket off once again and placed it on the hard, cold ground. Roger stretched out first, and then Arthur and Poopsie curled up on his jelly belly.

CHAPTER 5: EDDIE THE EAGLE

Merle the Squirrel remained high up in the big, old oak tree where Mr. Moon had left him at midnight. He knew he had no other choice because too many dangers lurked in the forest at nightfall.

He took a large, deep breath and thought about his conversation with Mr. Moon. Suddenly, the dark sky grew lighter and the stars grew brighter. "Mr. Moon is inside of me," he whispered to himself. "I don't have to be afraid. I'm a very powerful squirrel. I really am."

To pass the time, he counted and recounted all the nuts in both pails. It was so much easier now. He would put all his nuts in one pail and then transfer them to the other. After counting the nuts at least ten times, he noted that he had sixty-four left. He figured if he ate just four more, he would still have fifteen to give each of his friends.

So he ate four more nuts. Then, on a partially fed, sunken tummy, all alone in the vast forest and shivering from the cold, he curled up his little webbed feet and hands and went to sleep.

As he drifted off, he did not see all the fireflies surrounding the branch where he slept. The blinking lights on their tails served as beacons and the warmth of their bodies covered Merle like a soft, protective blanket.

Nor did he see Eddie the Eagle's roaming eyes searching the dense forest.

CHAPTER 6

RACCOON

Even though fast asleep, Merle the Squirrel heard something.
Something scary. And it awoke the little squirrel with a jolt.

Eyes fixed like buttons, he peered out into the forest. "What was
that?" he whispered to himself. The noise came from directly below
him at the base of the tree. He sucked in his breath and froze. He
had never felt so small and vulnerable in his entire life. What was he
going to do?

Standing as tall as he could with his little squirrel hands curled tightly
against his chest, he slowly rolled his eyes down. "Who's there?"
he asked in his bravest voice. But there was no answer. The noises
became more intense and seemed closer. "I said, who is there?" he
demanded a bit louder.

All of a sudden, Merle saw the masked villain through the tree branches.
His heart pounded as the beast approached him. "Leave me alone!" he
shouted. "I'm only a tiny squirrel. I can't defend myself!"

CHAPTER 6: RACCOON

The raccoon looked up and licked his lips. "All the better, my friend," he growled.

"Oh me, oh my. Oh me, oh my," said Merle as he paced back and forth on the big branch of the old oak tree, wringing his hands together.

He looked up into the sky in desperation. "Mr. Moon," he cried. "Mr. Moon, are you there? Please help me! The raccoon is going to eat me!"

At once he heard Mr. Moon's soothing voice whispering inside his head. "Remember what I said, little one. You are a very powerful squirrel because I am always with you."

His heart thumped so hard and so fast that he thought it might leap out of his chest. His pie eyes stared straight ahead. He was thinking... thinking...thinking.

Suddenly, he knew what to do. He quickly turned around and picked up his pail of nuts. The pail was heavy, but he managed to maneuver it onto the tree branch directly above the hungry raccoon.

"Don't come any closer, raccoon," he shouted, "or I'm going to let you have it!"

The raccoon snorted in response and continued to climb the tree.

"I mean it, raccoon. I don't want to hurt you, but I will if I have to."

"I'm hungry and I'm going to eat you, squirrel. You don't scare me."

"Here goes," said Merle as he took his first nut and hurled it as hard as he could at the raccoon. But he was so weak from hunger that it fell short of its target.

CHAPTER 6: RACCOON

"What are you doing, you stupid squirrel?" asked the raccoon. "Stop that at once."

Without hesitation, Merle pumped up his chest and shouted at the top of his little squirrel lungs, "I am not a stupid squirrel! I am a powerful squirrel!"

"You have no chance against me," grunted the raccoon as he continued to climb the tree.

Merle quickly grabbed the biggest nut he could find. Taking aim, he threw the nut so hard that he thought his little arm would fly out of its socket. But this nut found its target and hit the raccoon directly in his eye. The blow frightened him so much that he let go of the tree trunk, slid to the ground and knocked himself out cold on a big, old rock.

Merle could not believe his eyes. "Yeah! Yeah! Yeah!" he shouted at the top of his lungs as he jumped up and down with glee. "I did it! I did it! I did it!"

His heart swelled with pride as he strutted back and forth on the tree branch. "I'm a champion! I'm a champion! I'm a champion!" he declared over and over again. "Mr. Moon was right! He was really right!"

The clouds opened up and Mr. Moon's full brightness filled the sky. "Greetings, Merle the Squirrel!"

"I scared the raccoon away, Mr. Moon! Me, Merle the Squirrel! I really did it! I feel so powerful and great and important and big and brave and happy!"

Mr. Moon laughed heartily. "Well, my little brave one, if you feel powerful, then you will attract more circumstances that will make you feel powerful. If you feel good, you will attract more circumstances that will make you feel good. You see, your circumstances do not create your feelings; your feelings create your circumstances. That is the law of the forest. It is fair and it is consistent. The forest will treat you the way you deserve to be treated by following your example. So always do everything that makes you feel your best."

"What are 'laws', Mr. Moon?" asked Merle.

"Laws are universal truths that apply to all creatures of the forest equally and unconditionally. There are many laws to learn, but you will only learn a few in this lifetime."

"How many laws are there, Mr. Moon?"

"There are many, little one, and they are all timeless and perfect, just like you. Just remember, the forest will give you the very best it has to offer in every situation. Think of it as a mirror of your own thoughts and feelings. So guard your thoughts and feelings at all times. If you align them with mine, you will experience wonderful things.

You are a divine creature who has been given all the tools required to be the greatest and the happiest and the most fulfilled squirrel you could ever imagine."

When Mr. Moon dipped behind a big cloud and was seen no more, Merle pondered on how his life had suddenly changed. Deep down inside, he felt a stirring, a gentle nudge that somehow helped him understand some of the things Mr. Moon had said. In a most peculiar way, he almost felt as though he already knew these truths, but had just forgotten. In any case, and most importantly, he realized that he was the commander of his ship and fully intended to guide it to more fantastic things. And as he embraced the joyous anticipation of his new lease on life, he also knew that Mr. Moon would always be with him everywhere he went.

CHAPTER 6: RACCOON

Suddenly he heard a loud swoosh above him. He puffed up his chest and in the loudest voice he could muster cried, "Who is there? Who is there? I'm not afraid! Tell me who you are!"

But while he awaited the answer, a great and mighty talon swooped him off his feet. Sheltered under powerful wings, Merle looked up. "Wow! Is that you, Eddie the Eagle?"

Eddie gently set him down on the highest tree branch of the old oak tree. "It is," he answered with a smile. "And I have a big surprise for you, Merle the Squirrel."

"Wow! A surprise! What is it?"

"Why don't you turn around and see for yourself?"

"Freddie! Freddie! Freddie!" shrieked Merle.

Upon being reunited, the two little creatures hugged each other until they were exhausted.

Teary-eyed, but still in total darkness, Freddie cried out to his friend, "I'm so sorry. I'm so sorry. Please forgive me for being such a horrible friend. I love you, Merle the Squirrel. I really do. I love you."

"I love you too, Freddie. And I forgive you," answered Merle with giant tears of joy streaming down his dirty, little squirrel cheeks.

"There is much more I have to say to you before you forgive me," added Freddie. "I want you to know that I was really wrong in how I treated you. Although I didn't mean anything I said, I am positive that I still hurt you. I'm not sure why I said those things in the first place. Maybe I thought they were funny. Maybe they made me feel more important than you. Maybe I'm just really immature. Maybe

CHAPTER 6: RACCOON

I was trying to fit in with everybody else. I don't know, for sure. But what I do know is that I am so terribly, terribly sorry. I should have stood up for you, Merle. I should have stood up for what was right.

And I had no idea how cold and lonely and dangerous the forest was. I never once offered to help you collect the nuts. But as selfish as I was, you still called me your friend.

When I ask you to forgive me, it's not because I think I deserve it, Merle, it's because I want another chance to prove to you that I can be a good friend. So please forgive me. Please give me another chance."

Suddenly, Freddie saw a shadow that slowly changed into a faint outline. "Wait!" He blinked a few times while his eyes adjusted to the dim light. "I can see! I can see!" The little mouse danced in the moonlight. "The light's back on! The light's back on! Mr. Moon was right! He really was!" He grabbed Merle the Squirrel and hugged him with all his might. "Thank you! Thank you! Thank you!" he shouted to the sky. "Thank you, Mr. Moon! Thank you, Merle the Squirrel!"

Merle had no idea what Freddie the Mouse was talking about, but he didn't care because this was the happiest day of his entire life. His little squirrel heart was so full, he thought it was going to burst.

Bathed in the light of Mr. Moon, Freddie and Merle danced and skipped and twirled and jumped and laughed and shouted and cried with glee, until they couldn't catch their breath any longer.

Eddie the Eagle gently folded his wings around the two, excited creatures. "Both of you must get some rest now. It has been a long night for all of us."

"What do you mean, Eddie? Aren't you taking us back to our other friends?" asked Merle. "Aren't you?"

CHAPTER 6: RACCOON

"Roger and Poopsie and Arthur must finish the journey they have started. They have many lessons to learn along the way. In the mean time, you have my promise that you both will be safe."

The majestic eagle spread his heavenly wings and shot straight into the air. His magnificent radiance lit up the entire sky as he watched over his charge.

CHAPTER 7
MR. SUN AND MISS DANDELION

It was ten o'clock in the morning. Unbeknownst to the threesome, the shortest day of the year was upon them and the darkness would return in just six hours. Arthur woke up first and stretched his little mouse legs in every direction. He sensed that something had changed. Turning his head from right to left, from left to right, looking straight ahead and then behind, he shouted at the top of his lungs, "Mr. Sun's shift has started!"

Roger Earl of Henry snorted and drooled and opened one eye. "Uh, what's going on, Arthur? What's all the fuss about?"

"It's not dark anymore, Roger!" he cried.

Roger Earl of Henry shielded his eyes from the giant, yellow dome looking down at them and pointed. "Look over there, Poopsie. There's Mr. Sun. And he's, uh, smiling."

Poopsie tried to gather himself in the most dignified manner possible. He straightened his silk cataloons and smoothed out his whiskers.

CHAPTER 7: MR. SUN AND MISS DANDELION

Then he grabbed his soiled, creased jacket from the damp ground and immediately put it on. He quickly washed his face, and then standing taller than he had ever stood before, greeted Mr. Sun. "Good Morning, Mr. Sun. How are you this morning?"

"Hi, Mr. Sun," saluted Arthur with a wave.

"Uh, hello, Mr. Sun." Roger wiped the drool from his chin and removed his hat.

Mr. Sun acknowledged each of the threesome in a bold, officious tone. "Greetings and salutations, Roger Earl of Henry, Poopscapaleon Appotamus and Arthur the Mouse. What are you doing in the forest so early?"

"We are looking for Merle the Squirrel," answered Arthur. "He has our pail of nuts. Mr. Moon turned his light off and we got lost in the dark."

Mr. Sun's forehead furrowed and his smile disappeared. "Is this correct, Poopscapaleon?"

Poopsie tried to swallow, but his throat felt dry and scratchy. "Sir, that is not entirely correct." He looked at his feet. "We were, well, we were mean to Merle the Squirrel and Mr. Moon said we would not be able to see his light until we got rid of our guilt and shame. That is why we are looking for Merle the Squirrel. To make things right."

"What do you have to say about this, Roger Earl of Henry?" asked Mr. Sun.

Roger moved a pebble with his big toe. "We, uh, were wondering, sir, can you tell us how to find Merle the Squirrel so that we will be able to see in the dark again?" he asked in his low, low voice. "Uh, could you do that for us, Mr. Sun?"

CHAPTER 7: MR. SUN AND MISS DANDELION

Arthur climbed up Roger's back, around his neck and to the top of his head. "And don't forget about Freddie. We have to find Freddie."

The threesome stood before Mr. Sun like tattered soldiers awaiting their orders. Poopsie was a sight to behold. His broken, black spectacles hung on his face at an odd angle. His red and white flowered smoking jacket was soiled, stained and wet with mud. His silk cataloons were dirty and shredded. Roger's hat was squashed beyond recognition and his neck seemed to have completely disappeared into his sticky, dirty fur. Arthur's little mouse ears were creased with sleep and his whiskers were bent askew.

Roger wiped the drool from his mouth with the back of his paw. "Uh, sir, can you please help us find them?"

Poopsie squeezed his way forward. "Mr. Sun, with all due respect, I really, really beg your pardon, but the problem is that we won't be able to find Merle the Squirrel if we can't see in the dark. And Mr. Moon told us that we won't be able to see in the dark until we find Merle the Squirrel. That does not seem fair, does it? So we were wondering if you could help us find him during your shift, before it gets dark again."

Mr. Sun raised one eyebrow and contemplated the question. Finally, he peered down at the foursome with disdain. "I am far too busy to help you find Merle the Squirrel during my shift. In order to see again in the dark, you will first have to find Mr. Moon and plead your case with him. This issue has nothing to do with me."

Poopsie gathered his courage to address Mr. Sun. "But, sir, we cannot find Mr. Moon during your shift. We would not know where to look."

"Indeed," replied Mr. Sun. "But in that regard, I may be of some assistance."

CHAPTER 7: MR. SUN AND MISS DANDELION

Roger rubbed his shrunken belly. "Can't we have something to eat first? I'm so hungry."

Arthur tried his best to appear brave, but felt cold, dehydrated and weak. "Me, too," he whispered in a faint voice.

Mr. Sun narrowed his eyes. "Indeed," he replied. "Can you imagine how Merle the Squirrel or Freddie the Mouse must be feeling, if they haven't already been eaten by a creature of the forest? Or are you so self-absorbed that you are unaware, or even worse, unfeeling about their plight?"

The trio stood in silence.

"This is grave. Very grave," said Mr. Sun. "But for Merle the Squirrel's sake, and for Freddie the Mouse's sake alone, I will assist you. I will send the three of you on a journey. During your journey you will find food and drink. Along the way, you will be given nine clues to help you find Mr. Moon before the dark begins. The first thing you must do is choose a leader. I will give you fifteen minutes precisely to accomplish this while I get on with my duties. Then you must tell me whom you have chosen and the journey must begin. Is that clear?"

They nodded in unison as they watched Mr. Sun disappear behind a cloud.

Poopsie looked sternly at Roger and Arthur and didn't waste any time. "Look, you guys, I think I should be the leader. My tail is the longest and the two of you could hang on to it while we walk in the forest. And I am a hunter. I could forage food for us."

Roger pumped up his dirty chest with pride. "Uh, but I'm a bulldog. I'm the biggest and the strongest and the two of you could ride on my back. And I could fight for us, I mean, if I really had to."

CHAPTER 7: MR. SUN AND MISS DANDELION

Arthur jumped up and down excitedly. "What do you mean? I should be the leader because I am the tiniest. I could hide really easily. And I can run fast, too!"

And on and on it went for ten minutes as the threesome rallied for leadership.

Suddenly, in the most incomprehensible way, a dandelion turned slowly to face them. "You'll get nowhere at all with that attitude," it stated in a very fast, high-pitched voice.

"Uh, what?" Roger bent over as low as he could go and peered inquisitively at the talking flower. "Did you say something?"

The dandelion lifted its brilliant, yellow head, looked directly at Roger and continued to speak. "Why don't you put your egos aside for a moment and draw straws? The clock is ticking, you know?"

Poopsie's whiskers quivered, his pupils dilated and his fur ruffled as he walked a full circle around the dandelion. "That is impossible. Dandelions do not talk."

"Well," the dandelion replied, "perhaps you have just not ever heard one. All living things communicate. Perhaps at a frequency that you cannot hear all the time, but nonetheless, we do speak. We not only communicate with each other, we also communicate with our neighbors. Sometimes we use electrical impulses to speak. Sometimes we use chemicals. How do you think we defend ourselves? And I dare say, Mr. Appotamus, you would not believe all the other commotion going on around you that even you cannot perceive with your acute senses."

Poopsie crouched down until his belly rested on the cool, damp ground and looked the dandelion in the eyes. "How do you know my name, dandelion?"

CHAPTER 7: MR. SUN AND MISS DANDELION

"To be perfectly honest, the forest has no secrets, Mr. Appotamus. And ours is a secretive and mysterious world. But we are all joined together as one."

Arthur walked up to the flower and peered at it. "Miss Dandelion, may I just say that you are ever so pretty. I've never taken the time to really look at a dandelion before. Your hair is even brighter than Mr. Sun and your stem seems so velvety smooth. Why haven't I heard a member of your family speak before?"

"Freddie the Mouse, every living creature communicates at a different frequency. Some higher, some lower. But that's neither here nor there. Who's going to be the leader? Shall I choose?"

"Uh, okay," said Roger. "Our time is running out. You choose one."

"Very well. I shall choose Poopscapaleon Appotamus. Now go tell Mr. Sun that you have a leader." Without saying good-bye, the dandelion turned away.

In precisely fifteen minutes, Mr. Sun peeked from behind the clouds and then emerged fully and brightly. "Well?" he demanded. "Who is going to be the leader?"

Poopsie stepped forward and tried to grab his tail, which kept swishing around uncontrollably. "I am the leader, sir."

"Very well. Your journey to find Mr. Moon will now begin. As I said before, you will find clues along the way as well as food and water. Are you ready?"

Poopsie finally grabbed hold of his long, black tail. "Yes, sir. We are ready."

CHAPTER 7: MR. SUN AND MISS DANDELION

"You must take ten steps south and then twenty steps east. On that exact spot, you will discover the path you must follow to find Mr. Moon. You will also locate food and water. Eat and drink until you are full as you have a very long and challenging journey ahead. You must find Mr. Moon before my shift ends, or once again, you will find yourself in the dark."

"Yes, sir," replied Poopsie with a lame salute. "Thank you, sir."

Mr. Sun nodded his head. "Then be off with you," he said in a most serious manner. "Good day."

CHAPTER 8

MR. TOAD

So Poopsie, Roger and Arthur ventured deep into the forest in search of food, water and their first clue to finding Mr. Moon. Poopsie led the group, with Roger holding on to Poopsie's tail and Arthur sitting atop Roger's head, peering from under his funny looking, red and white checkered hat.

"Okay, heads' up, you guys," said Poopsie. "Ten steps south and twenty steps east."

"Uh, so which way is south?" asked Roger.

"Well, Mr. Sun's shift starts in the east and ends in the west. So this way must be south." Poopsie pointed to his left.

Like a short train, with Roger's stubby tail following like a caboose, they took ten steps south and stopped.

"That's east! That's east!" shouted Arthur as he pointed to the right, while trying to give his best team effort.

CHAPTER 8: MR. TOAD

"Okay, mouse brain," replied Poopsie. "Let's go."

Once again the threesome measured out twenty steps, carefully navigating the dense foliage, and headed east.

When they arrived on the designated spot, they found a twenty-foot wide, fresh water stream that stretched as far as the eye could see from left to right. Its clear, blue water reflected the rich colors of the surrounding landscape.

"Look over there!" exclaimed Arthur, who pointed to an opening in the forest on the other side of the stream. "There it is! There's the path Mr. Sun was talking about!"

"That can't be the path Mr. Sun was talking about, mouse head," replied Poopsie as he looked around. "How are we supposed to get there? The stream looks like it divides the forest in half. There must be another path on this side somewhere."

Roger paid no attention to the path. Instead, he ogled the stream and its beckoning, cool water. "I'm so thirsty." He awkwardly lowered his rotund body to the slippery grass and then dragged himself on his belly, inch-by-inch, paw-by-paw, towards the stream.

Poopsie squinted at Roger. "Why are you dragging your belly through the grass like that? You look utterly ridiculous."

"Leave him alone," ordered Arthur who was spread eagle between Roger's ears. "You know he's deathly afraid of water. He can't swim, you know? Why do you have to be such a bully?"

Poopsie sighed. Rather than start a brawl with Arthur and use up any energy he had left, he decided to quench his thirst instead. He raced to the edge of the stream, crouched down and then unabashedly dipped his paw into the water to check the temperature. Finding it neither too hot nor too cold, he began to drink.

When Roger finally found his courage to approach the edge of the water, he rested for a minute to catch his breath.

"You are really something, Roger," chided Poopsie again. "First of all, you're afraid of water, and second, you're so fat that you can't even crawl on your belly without practically having a heart attack. And you wanted to be the leader?"

"Shut up!" screamed Arthur. "Don't you have a heart? Just shut up."

"Don't you raise your voice to me, you little pin head," yelled Poopsie. "I'm your leader and don't you forget it," he shouted.

An unfamiliar voice stopped the argument. "So drink to your hearts' content, but just keep your voices down, will you? You are scaring all the flies away, for goodness sakes," croaked the chubby, warty, old toad who was sitting on a shaded rock by the stream. "Just have your drink and then be on your way."

Poopsie's fur stood on end and his tail swished back and forth. Adjusting his broken, black spectacles, which had lost a lens along the way, he eyed the toad suspiciously. "We've had a very long day, toad. Are you here to trick us or to help us?"

"Neither. Just drink to your hearts' content and go away. I want to be left alone in peace," replied the stubby-bodied toad in a cantankerous tone.

Too dehydrated and weak to argue with the crotchety toad, the threesome stood side by side at the edge of the stream, and for the first time in a very long time, drank water until fully satisfied.

CHAPTER 8: MR. TOAD

"Uh, Mr. Toad?" said Roger with copious amounts of water dripping from his jowls. "Can you help us find Mr. Moon?"

"Hmmm," said the toad. "Let me think." He eyeballed a small berry hidden in the grass and, with a quick flick of his tongue, deposited the juicy treat into his mouth.

"Well?" asked Poopsie impatiently. "Can you help us?"

The toad stared into space for a moment through his big, bulging eyes. "I suppose I can."

"Well? What do you have to say then?" Poopsie persisted. "We don't have all day, you know?"

Unmoved by Poopsie's tone, the toad contemplated his answer as he sat peacefully on his favorite rock. "The way to find Mr. Moon," he finally replied, "is by following the path on the other side of the stream."

The threesome looked across the water in unison and stared at the path, which ran perpendicular to the stream.

"Uh, you mean over there?" Roger said, while pointing across the water.

"Yes, over there," the toad answered matter-of-factly.

Totally aggravated by his response, Poopsie hissed, "Well, you stupid toad, how do we get to the other side of the stream?"

"It's very simple, really. The stream stretches as far as the eye can see, so you will have to cross it to get to the path. There is no other way."

"There must be another way, toad head! There must be a path somewhere on this side of the stream!"

CHAPTER 8: MR. TOAD

"Nope," answered the toad.

Poopsie's eyes became slits. "Well, how deep is the stream? I can't see the bottom. Arthur's afraid of water. Roger can't swim. And I have no intention of getting dirty."

"Then you have a real dilemma because the stream is very, very deep. The stream is as deep as it is wide."

Upon hearing this comment, Roger became extremely upset. His big, old body started to tremble and shiver and shake. "But I can't swim, Mr. Toad. I can't."

"Who said anything about swimming?" retorted the toad as he stared at the trio through dark, unblinking eyes.

Poopsie stepped forward and carefully kept a safe distance from the stocky, warty amphibian. "Look, toad brain, I'm the leader of this group and therefore I am fully responsible for them. It is of the utmost importance that we find Mr. Moon. If you cannot help us, then for Petie's sakes, just lead us to someone who can. Time is of the essence."

"Hmmm," said the toad as he eyeballed another berry in the grass. "It's very clear to me that you will have to cross the stream if you want to find Mr. Moon."

Poopsie clenched his teeth. "If we cannot swim across the stream, how to you propose we get to the other side?"

And on that note, the toad leaped off the rock and slowly and deliberately walked across the stream until he reached the other side. His short, hind legs seemed to support his chubby body on top of the water. Then he ran a zigzag path back to the threesome and settled once again on his favorite rock. "You see? That's how you do it."

CHAPTER 8: MR. TOAD

Roger's eyeballs almost jumped out of their sockets. He shook his head a few times, his jowls spraying everyone and everything with spit, blinked a few times and shook his head again. "Uh, am I seeing things?"

Poopsie extended his neck to look more closely at the toad. "How do you do that, toad? Is that some sort of a trick?"

His intelligent eyes riveted on the trio. "Hmmm," he said. "Yes, I suppose for all intents and purposes it is a trick. You see, your brain does not know the difference between what is real and what is not. It is merely a sophisticated movie reel that projects thought images onto a big screen through your senses."

Poopsie, Roger and Arthur all squinted as they listened intently.

"Can you explain it in more simple terms, toad?" asked Poopsie impatiently.

"That's about as simple as it gets. There is really nothing more to it. What you see through your eyes is a mirror image of your thoughts. The memory bank of your brain puts everything together in a form you can clearly see and understand. If you want to change your reality, you must change your thoughts. It's a simple concept, but one that's rather difficult to master, I'm afraid. Most entities make it far more complex than it is and then fail miserably at making it work."

Suddenly Roger felt uncomfortable in his own skin. "Oh, geez. I don't feel so good."

"Well, what we see is what we see, toad brain," shouted Poopsie, who was getting extremely agitated.

"Not necessarily," replied the amphibian in an unperturbed manner. "You don't see my tail, do you?"

CHAPTER 8: MR. TOAD

"Uh, tail?" muttered Roger.

"Yes, my tail. Can you see it?"

"Toads don't have tails. Don't be ridiculous," scoffed Poopsie.

"I do. I have a tail. You just can't see it."

The threesome formed a circle around the toad and examined him closely.

"We don't see a tail, Mr. Toad," said Arthur.

"That doesn't mean I don't have one. You just can't see it." And on that note, he climbed up a tree and suspended himself from a branch with, what appeared to be, an invisible rope.

"See," he shouted while hanging upside down. "I'm hanging by my tail."

"Come down here right now," demanded Poopsie. "Right now!"

So the toad dropped from the tree branch and landed on his favorite shaded rock by the stream.

"Uh, why can't we see your tail, Mr. Toad?" asked Roger.

"You can't see it because no one has ever seen a toad with a tail. There is no such information in your memory banks, so my tail does not exist in your realm of information. You see, you don't see with your eyes, you see with your brain, which transfers information from your mind and your thoughts and your beliefs. Your eyes and other senses are just the mechanism you use to experience your beliefs. If you believe what I say, then you will eventually see my tail. It's just that simple."

CHAPTER 8: MR. TOAD

Poopsie pointed his finger and raised his voice. "Listen, toad breath! All we want to do is find Mr. Moon. And to find Mr. Moon, we have to cross the stream. And to cross the stream, we have to somehow walk across the water without falling through. We certainly don't have time to listen to your drivel."

"It certainly isn't drivel," replied the toad. "Just believe you can walk across the stream and you will. If I can do it, you can do it. You'll find a way."

"Uh, Mr. Toad, how exactly does that work?"

He ogled Roger for a full minute through his bulging eyes. "Suffice it to say it just does, bulldog. Does it matter how a caterpillar changes into a butterfly? Do not waste time with complexities. If it works, it works! That is all you need to know. Just find a way to believe you can do it and you will."

So the threesome huddled together to plan their next move.

"Uh, I can't do this," whimpered Roger. "I'll fall right through the water. I will, you know. I'm heavy. And I can't swim."

"I'll drown for sure," wailed Arthur. "Please don't make me do it, Poopsie," he pleaded with his little mouse voice.

Poopsie looked at the two sternly. "Heads' up, team. Time is running out. If that ugly, old toad can walk across the stream, so can we. I'll go first. Arthur, you ride on top of my back. If anything goes wrong, I can swim, so we'll both be safe. When we get to the other side, it'll be your turn, Roger. And don't argue with me. I have no intention of spending another night in the dark."

Suddenly, Poopsie's whiskers began to twitch and his mouth began to salivate. He stuck his nose high in the air. "Food!" he shouted. "I smell food! It's on the other side!"

Streams of drool formed at Roger's mouth as he, too, smelled the buffet of tuna, liver and cheese.

"Oh, wow!" exclaimed Arthur. "I smell cheese!"

Poopsie stood as tall as he could and pumped up his chest. "Okay, men, this is what we have to do. First, Arthur, you must jump on my back and hold on tightly."

So Arthur the Mouse jumped on Poopsie's back and gripped the collar of his dirty, shredded smoking jacket.

"Okay, then. So far, so good. Here's the way we are going to do this. We are going to close our eyes. If we don't see the water, then we can trick out brains into thinking we are walking across ice."

Roger trembled at the thought. He had never been so afraid in his life. "Uh, I'm not sure."

Poopsie grabbed him by the ear and pulled hard. "Look, dog breath, once you see me do it, then you'll be able to do it, too. Keep your thoughts focused on those meaty kibbles on the other side of the stream and pretend the water is frozen. Have you ever walked on ice, Roger?"

"Well, yeah," he answered skeptically. "But it was real ice."

"Never mind those minor details right now, okay? When you close your eyes, I want you to imagine walking across ice."

Weak with hunger, Roger sat his big, bulldog rump down on the grass and obeyed. "Okay."

CHAPTER 8: MR. TOAD

"Great," said Poopsie in his bravest voice. "Are we ready, Arthur?"

The little mouse could hear his heart thumping wildly in his chest. "Ready, I think," he answered in a wee, wee voice.

"Close your eyes, Arthur," Poopsie ordered.

With his nose moist with the anticipation of devouring the feast of tuna awaiting him on the other side, Poopsie closed his eyes and visualized an immense, frozen stream before him. "Here we go!"

Without any further hesitation, he ran across the stream as fast as he could. Once on the other side, he leaped into the air in triumph with arms widespread in victory. "Touchdown!"

"We did it! We did it!" screamed Arthur. "We really did it!"

Poopsie dropped to his knees, kissed the ground and then quickly turned to Roger. "I see a big, big bowl of your favorite kibbles over here, my man! Okay, big boy, close your eyes and come and get it!"

Roger reluctantly arose. His stomach felt queasy and his skin felt prickly and cold. "Uh, what kind of kibbles are they, Poopsie?"

"They're your favorite kind! Liver!"

"Uh, oh boy. I'm so hungry."

When he closed his eyes, the smell of liver wafted through the air and into his big, black nose. His nostrils flared and he began to salivate. He was so hungry that he would let nothing stand between himself and his next meal.

So Roger Earl of Henry took a deep breath, closed his eyes and ran across the stream until he felt the cool grass under his feet.

"Yah! Yah! Yah!" hollered Arthur. "We all did it! We really did it! We ran across the stream!"

The toad, who stood by watching, clapped his little, webbed hands. "Absolutely fantastic," he exclaimed. "You see, you did it! You must clearly understand what I say in order to find Mr. Moon. And what I say is this: your thoughts, your feelings and your beliefs determine your reality. That is the law and I have spoken. Go eat now, my friends, to your hearts' content. You are on the right path."

Then the toad hopped off his favorite rock and disappeared into the forest with his curly tail following behind.

The trio ate and ate and ate until their stomachs ached with fullness, then skipped down the path with satisfied tummies and a new and most interesting way of looking at life.

CHAPTER 9

CLAUDIA, THE SPIDER

The threesome walked for an hour without finding any more clues in their search for Mr. Moon.

"We'd better find something fast," said Poopsie. "Mr. Sun won't be here for long."

"Well, uh, what are we looking for?" asked Roger in his low, low voice.

"Who knows?" replied Poopsie. "After the toad and the dandelion, nothing would surprise me. Keep your eyes open."

Suddenly they heard a wee, wee voice coming from inside the forest. "Excuse me? Excuse me?"

They stopped and turned towards the small, but commanding voice. "Who goes there?" asked Poopsie in his loudest, meanest, leader voice.

A tiny spider, about half an inch long, crossed their path and stopped in

CHAPTER 9: CLAUDIA, THE SPIDER

front of Poopsie. Two red triangles formed the shape of an hourglass on the underside of her shiny, black, spherical abdomen. The arachnid walked on eight jointed legs with claws at the end of each.

"Are you the leader?" she asked.

Poopsie recoiled at the mere thought of a teeny spider speaking to him. He leaned over to look at the spider. "That's right. I'm the leader."

She stared intensely at Poopsie and blinked a few times. "Are you sure you're the leader?"

"What? Of course I am sure. Why would I say I was if I was not?"

"You were not supposed to be the leader at all. At all." The spider shook her head again and again and again.

Roger pushed Poopsie aside. "Uh, Miss Spider, we're trying to find Mr. Moon before Mr. Sun's shift ends. Can you help us?"

The spider appraised Roger with her eight eyes. "I suppose I can, but you are not going to find Mr. Moon if Poopscapaleon is the leader. No way."

Poopsie straightened his filthy, red and white flowered smoking jacket and ironed out the creases with his paws. He pulled up his white, silk cataloons, adjusted his broken, black spectacles and stuck his nose as close to the spider as possible. "How dare you talk to me like that, you stupid, little spider."

She quickly crawled up Poopsie's leg, around his neck and up to the top of his head.

"Stop that!" Poopsie shook his head, but the spider hung on tightly with her claws.

CHAPTER 9: CLAUDIA, THE SPIDER

"I said stop that right now! I could wipe you out with one swipe of my paw!"

The spider crawled down to the tip of Poopsie's nose and looked at him directly in the eyes. She revealed two small fangs on either side of her mouth and replied, "And I could kill you with one drop of my venom, Mr. Appotamus, for I, Claudia, am a black widow."

Poopsie's eyes opened like saucers and he stood as still as a statue while looking at the small, but deadly spider sitting at the tip of his bright, pink nose.

"Do I have your attention now?" she asked. "As you know, felines are particularly susceptible to my venom."

Poopsie blinked once and his comrades remained silent.

"Good."

Unperturbed by the drama unfolding, Arthur the Mouse slowly walked up to Poopsie and stared at the spider who was anchored at the end of his nose. "Miss Black Widow, my name is Arthur. Gosh, I have never seen such a beautiful spider up so close. Spiders always run away from me. If you don't mind me saying, your colors are so very striking. You look like a fine piece of jewelry."

"Thank you, Arthur," she replied while holding Poopsie's gaze. "And you are a very striking mouse. You may call me Claudia, if you wish."

Not at all used to compliments in his circle of friends, Arthur turned the color of a beet. "Oh, gosh! Thank you so much, Claudia."

Roger, who knew he was not as susceptible to the black widow's

CHAPTER 9: CLAUDIA, THE SPIDER

venom, moved closer. "Miss Black Widow, uh, would it be possible to help us find Mr. Moon?"

"As I said before, Roger Earl of Henry, you are not going to find Mr. Moon if Poopscapaleon Appotamus is the leader."

Not able to contain himself any longer, Poopsie hissed, "I was appointed leader by the dandelion and I have every intention of fulfilling my post!"

"Indeed," said the black widow spider as she held eye contact with Poopsie. "But as of now, you are no longer the leader because I hereby appoint Arthur the Mouse to the position."

Arthur gasped. "Why me, Claudia?"

"Just because," she answered matter-of-factly. "If you want to find Mr. Moon, then you will have to be the leader, Arthur the Mouse."

Totally unprepared for this turn of events, Poopsie screamed, "Why Arthur? I mean, why him? He's just a teeny mouse. I am a cat! I just directed my team to walk across a stream, for Petie's sakes."

The black widow let out a long sigh and crawled down to the ground. "Why is it so very important to you that you are the leader?"

"Because," he shouted. "I like being the leader! It makes me feel important!"

The spider winced at Poopsie's outburst. "Why is it," she asked again, "that you want to set yourself apart from everybody else when you are certainly no different than the forsaken alley cats who roam the earth in darkness?"

CHAPTER 9: CLAUDIA, THE SPIDER

Poopsie pumped up his chest and adjusted his spectacles. "But I don't roam the earth in darkness. I live in a castle, black widow. I am the only one out of a huge litter who lives in a castle."

"Poopscapaleon Appotamus! Importance cannot be measured by our title, or by the type of house we live in, or by the type of clothes we wear, or by our circumstances. I live under a rock, have no title and have no clothes, but I could kill you with just one drop of my venom. My species has been on this planet for over three hundred million years, but we don't consider ourselves superior in any way. We understand that each creature has its equal place in the forest and we respect that."

"You don't understand, spider. I need to be the leader," Poopsie implored unabashedly.

"Not one of us has any reason to need anything at all. All our needs have already been met. The forest is abundant and there is more than enough in it for everybody. It will supply everything you ask for on demand, with absolutely no conditions placed on you, or on me, or on anybody else. Quite simply, the forest mirrors anything and everything you dwell upon. Needing is a sign of lack. So at this very moment you are drawing more lack into your life, Mr. Appotamus. Not a good trait for a leader, don't you agree? If you want to find Mr. Moon, you will have to show humility. So are you willing to step down from your leadership role and let a mouse lead you the rest of the way?"

Poopsie looked at Roger who was rolling a pebble around with his big toe. "Roger? Do you agree with that?"

In a very, very faint voice, Roger replied, "Uh, I don't know."

"You don't know? You don't know? What do you mean you don't know?" He then looked at Arthur who was hiding behind Roger.

CHAPTER 9: CLAUDIA, THE SPIDER

"Arthur? What do you have to say about this?"

"Nothing," said Arthur in his little mouse voice.

Poopsie pumped up his chest, perked up his ears, spread out his whiskers and paced one way and then the other with his paws behind his back. "Wasn't I appointed the leader? Wasn't I?"

"Uh, well, you were appointed, not nominated," said Roger hesitantly.

Poopsie glared at Roger. "Who do you think you are talking to, dog breath? Didn't I get you across the stream?"

The black widow positioned herself between the three. "Poopscapaleon Appotamus, there is no further point for discussion. The only way you are going to find Mr. Moon is by showing humility. We are all equal in his eyes. That is the law and I have spoken. So is Arthur the Mouse leading the team now, or do you prefer to be in the dark forever?"

And so it was. The case was closed.

Off they went in search of their next clue with Arthur in the lead, Roger next and a very dejected, ousted leader shuffling silently behind.

CHAPTER 10

MRS. ROBIN

"Look! Mr. Sun has moved halfway across the sky! The day is almost over!" exclaimed Arthur in his newly found role as leader.

"I'm, uh, going as fast as I can," replied Roger.

Poopsie, who was still reeling from taking orders from a spider, soundlessly trailed the others with his coal, black tail hanging limply between the legs of his dirty, silk cataloons.

One hill led to another as the path carved its way through the dense forest. As the leafage of the giant trees began to block out most of the remaining light of Mr. Sun, the surroundings became more uninviting and ominous. In fact, the dark green foliage of the twisted tree branches became so thick that the trees seemed to form a maze, rather than just an ordinary forest.

But it wasn't just an ordinary forest, was it? What ordinary forest would inhabit creatures and flowers that could talk? What ordinary forest would hold nine clues leading to Mr. Moon?

CHAPTER 10: MRS. ROBIN

And Mr. Moon was not just an ordinary moon either, was he? He was both a mysterious and elusive entity.

At this juncture, it would be appropriate to note that, while admiring Mr. Moon's positive traits, one could not help but realize that he was much more than just a moon. In fact, at this point in time, it would be prudent to note that Mr. Moon was not only just a moon, but also the forest...and everything in it.

"Come on, you guys," yelled Arthur in his biggest mouse voice. "Pay attention! We don't want to miss anything!"

But for another hour, they heard nothing except their own footsteps.

Roger pointed to the sky. "Look! Mr. Sun has moved some more!"

"Just keep going," said Arthur. "We have no time to lose!"

As Mr. Sun's light began to fade, the air started to cool rapidly. Poopsie buttoned his smoking jacket, which barely fit over his enormous belly. Roger pulled his funny looking hat tightly over his ears and sheltered Arthur, whose little, beady eyes peered out like shiny, black marbles.

The trio began to tread more slowly now as it became increasingly difficult to see in the dim light. Poopsie, who was too proud to admit he was terribly afraid of the dark, grabbed hold of Roger's stubby tail as the forest became darker by the minute.

"Are you guys, uh, getting scared, or is it just me?" asked Roger.

Poopsie's eyes shone like emeralds in the impending nightfall as he searched the forest for clues. "Just keep going, dog breath. There's no time to be afraid."

CHAPTER 10: MRS. ROBIN

Suddenly, a little voice was heard in the distance. "Help! Help! Help!"

"What's that?" said Arthur, turning his little mouse ear to the sound.

Roger's ears perked up. "Uh, did you hear that, Poopsie? Somebody is calling out for help."

Poopsie stopped for a moment, then answered quickly, "Come on, you wimp heads. Just keep going, for Petie's sakes! We don't have time for any unexpected detours unless, of course, you never want to see in the dark ever again!"

"Help! Help!" the fragile voice called out again. "Someone, please help me!"

Roger stopped dead in his tracks and pointed to a pile of logs a short distance away. "There! It's coming from there!"

"Help me! Oh, please!"

Poopsie stood his ground. "I said, COME ON, sawdust brains," he urged. "We don't have time to investigate! The day is more than half over!"

Roger stepped off the path with Arthur tucked under his hat and followed the panicked cries that pierced the forest. About ten feet into the thick foliage, they saw a robin trapped under a large, fallen branch.

"Look," cried Arthur as they moved closer. "There she is!"

"Uh, what's wrong, robin?" asked Roger as he peered down at the entangled, little bird.

CHAPTER 10: MRS. ROBIN

The robin lifted her weary head, revealing her crimson breast. The white rings around her eyes seemed to glow like miniature headlights. "I'm stuck and I can't get out!" she exclaimed. "If I don't get out, a hungry raccoon will eat me! My babies are waiting for me in our nest and I have to feed them soon or they will die, too!" Soft tears flowed down her delicate cheeks.

"Oh, don't cry, Mrs. Robin," consoled Arthur. "We'll help you. Don't worry."

In the distance, Poopsie rolled his paws into fists and shouted at the top of his cat lungs, "Come on, lame brains! We don't have time for this! If we don't go, then we will be the ones eaten by a hungry raccoon!" He started to walk down the path and waved for them to follow.

"Oh, please, Poopscapaleon Appotamus!" pleaded the robin. "Please come back and help me!"

He scrunched up his face for a moment in quiet contemplation and then turned towards the robin. "No, robin! We can't help you! We're running out of time and we have to find Mr. Moon!"

"Oh, my," she lamented. "My babies are so hungry, and the forest is full of scavengers. I was trying to capture a beetle grub as fast as I could and I carelessly slipped my leg under this twig. I think it might be broken. Oh, my!"

"Uh, well, don't you worry, Mrs. Robin, Arthur and I will help you," said Roger. But when he looked at the large branch that trapped the robin's leg, he realized that it was far too heavy for a bulldog and a mouse to move. "Uh, come on, Poopsie. We need your help. We can't move this tree branch alone."

"Hurry," yelled Arthur. "She's worried about her babies!"

CHAPTER 10: MRS. ROBIN

But Poopsie dug his heels into the cold, wet dirt as he looked behind him. "No! We have to find Mr. Moon before Mr. Sun's shift ends!"

The robin turned her weakened body towards Poopsie. "Please have mercy on me," she whispered. "If not for me, then for my babies."

Poopsie felt his heart thumping in his chest as his anxiety level increased. "No!" he shouted back defiantly.

Roger and Arthur turned to Poopsie who stood his ground with his arms crossed. "Are you saying that you are willing to let Mrs. Robin and her babies die?" asked Arthur.

Poopsie straightened his red and white flowered smoking jacket and crossed his arms again. "No, that's not what I'm saying, pea heads. What I'm saying is that we have to make a choice. Either we leave the robin behind and find Mr. Moon before Mr. Sun's shift ends, or we stay and risk not ever being able to see in the dark again. To me, it makes sense to keep going. Somebody else will come around soon enough and help the robin."

"Uh, but she will surely die, Poopsie," said Roger Earl of Henry. "There's no one else around to help her. And if she dies, so will her babies. I'm not sure I want to explain that to Mr. Moon when we find him. And you know, uh, what he said, Poopsie. He said that he knows everything that goes on in the forest down to the whereabouts of the smallest sparrow."

"And treating Merle the Squirrel poorly made him mad enough," added Arthur. "How do you think he will feel if Mrs. Robin and her babies die on account of us?"

Poopsie thought hard for a few moments. "All right! All right! I'll help, for Petie's sakes. We're just wasting time talking about this

CHAPTER 10: MRS. ROBIN

anyway." He turned his eyes towards the robin. "This better not take long, robin, or I will hold you responsible. I will, you know."

So Poopsie rushed back and looked down at the helpless, little bird. Upon seeing her up close, he could see the bruises around her delicate leg and the drops of blood pooling under her. He could see the sadness in her eyes and the defeat in her limp feathers. Poopsie had never seen this kind of suffering before.

As he moved even closer, she stared up at him for a moment and then bowed her head in total surrender. Did she think he was going to eat her?

Poopsie suddenly felt an unexpected and very peculiar feeling in the pit of his stomach. What was this odd sensation? It felt as though a great rush of air was escaping from his stomach to his chest, and then from his chest to his throat. The force was so severe, that he fell on one knee and involuntarily made a weird, whimpering sound. He grabbed his throat with both hands, but the pressure grew stronger as this strange feeling continued to travel through his head to the back of his eyes. Finally, when his eyes began to feel moist, Poopsie grabbed the sides of his head and doubled over. What was happening to him? What was going on? Was he dying?

Turning his focus back to the robin, he thought about how afraid she must have felt, all alone in the night. She must have been in so much pain. If they had not come around, she could have died. Her babies would never have known what had happened to her. How long would they have lived without food? How would they have felt, all alone in the dark forest? Would they have survived the night or would a hungry predator have eaten them? He shuddered at the thought.

Lost in his own world, Poopsie didn't hear Roger shout his name.

"Poopsie," he shouted again. "Uh, snap out of it. We need your help."

CHAPTER 10: MRS. ROBIN

Finally getting Poopsie's full attention, Roger continued. "Okay, men, on my count let's lift the branch from her leg. Uh, and make sure you are gentle. We don't want to hurt her. One, two, three..." They carefully heaved the large branch from her tiny leg.

"Is it broken?" fretted Arthur. "Can you move it, Mrs. Robin?"

"Oh, dear, let me see." The tired robin lifted her leg and a big smile came over her face. "It's fine! It's fine!"

"But it's bleeding," said Roger. "We have to, uh, stop the bleeding or you will die."

Poopsie bent over and gave the bottom cuff of his white, silk cataloons a tug, tearing a strip all around his pant leg. "Here! Here! Use this!"

Roger gently applied the silk bandage to the robin's injured leg and tied a loose knot. "There you go, Mrs. Robin. That should stop the bleeding and, uh, keep the wound clean until it heals up."

Peering down at Mrs. Robin, who was clearly mended for the time being, Poopsie felt utter relief that she would survive the ordeal. For the first time in his life, he actually felt like he had done something decent, something thoughtful, and something unselfish. His actions not only saved the lives of Mrs. Robin and her babies, but they also made him feel light, and airy and giddy inside. It would be rather difficult to describe these feelings in words, so he decided to keep his thoughts to himself.

Mrs. Robin affectionately looked at the three with tears in her eyes. "You have been so kind. My babies will be safe because of you. I know you are on a very important journey and you still took the time to help a stranger like me."

"Are you sure you're okay, Mrs. Robin?" asked Arthur.

CHAPTER 10: MRS. ROBIN

She gently flew a full circle around the trio and then landed atop a tree stump nearby. "Yes! I'm okay! I must hurry now and go to my nest. Since the three of you have demonstrated such kindness by stopping to assist me, I will gladly lead you to your next signpost. It's only a few minutes away."

Arthur jumped up and down with delight. "Oh, thank you so much, Mrs. Robin!"

"Hurry," she urged as she flew into the sky. "Follow me! And remember, to find Mr. Moon, you must show compassion. The act of compassion is more powerful than you think. It reinforces our connection with one another and can heal anything and everything. By showing compassion to others, you may even find that you heal yourself. That is the law and I have spoken."

The three quickly followed the robin and went forward to seek their next clue.

CHAPTER 11

MR. MOLE

"Here it is! Good luck, my friends, and thank you," said the robin as she disappeared into the thick forest.

"Uh, I don't see anything, do you?" asked Roger as he looked around.

Poopsie adjusted his black spectacles and squinted. "Mr. Sun's shift is almost over and it's getting harder and harder to see."

"Mrs. Robin wouldn't, uh, lie to us. It must be here somewhere."

"We still have six signposts to go, for Petie's sakes," hissed Poopsie. "We're never going to make it on time. I think we're up against a brick wall."

"Uh, let's just walk ahead a bit. Maybe it's just around the corner."

"Look, sawdust brain, I'm hungry and I'm tired. I say we just cut our

CHAPTER 11: MR. MOLE

losses and try to find our way back. It'll take less time than groping our way through this dismal forest and we might even make it home before dark."

"What about Merle the Squirrel?" asked Arthur. "What will happen to him? Or Freddie?"

"What will happen to any of us if we get lost in the dark?" yelled Poopsie, who was clearly getting more and more upset.

"Why do you have to be so negative?" asked Roger. "Uh, we're just wasting time, you know? Why don't we just keep walking? Besides, it's not like we have any choice if we want to see in the dark ever again."

"I'm in charge and I say we keep going," added Arthur.

"What for?" shouted Poopsie who felt he was on the brink of a major anxiety attack. "To spend another night in the dark? You have no idea what dangers lurk in this forest, do you? Besides, we haven't eaten for hours. And look at me, for Petie's sakes. I'm a mess."

Arthur and Roger stared at Poopsie. Once immaculate in his appearance, he was now disheveled and dirty. His red and white flowered smoking jacket looked unkempt, untidy and slovenly. His white cataloons, which were now missing half of one leg, were tattered and torn. His messy, muddy, matted fur stuck up every which way.

"Why don't we, uh, just vote," suggested Roger. "Everybody who wants to go on, raise their hand."

Arthur and Roger raised their hands. Poopsie stuck his hands in his pockets.

"That's it, then," said Arthur. "We keep going."

CHAPTER 11: MR. MOLE

"Meeeeow," argued Poopsie crankily. "The darker it gets, the harder it will be to keep on the path. We're either going to starve to death or get eaten. We're up against a brick wall, I say, a brick wall."

But despite Poopsie's negativity about a good outcome, the trio cautiously proceeded down the path.

In just a few minutes, they stood dumbfounded by a most peculiar sight.

Looking completely out of place, square in the middle of the path, sat a small, plump, short-tailed mole behind a giant desk. Magnifying his tiny, beady eyes to grotesque dimensions, a pair of black rimmed glasses rested on his flat, pointed snout and seemed to hang on his head from invisible ears. In one of his five-toed feet, he held a long, fat cigarette, which sent thick, blue smoke high into the sky. He muttered to himself amid a flurry of papers and books and notepads that were stacked high around him like a fortress.

If that wasn't bazaar enough, behind the furry, gray mammal and his enormous desk stood a solid, red, brick wall that extended vertically and horizontally as far as the eye could see.

"Hello?" said Poopsie. "Mr. Mole?"

The mole continued smoking and reading and muttering and shuffling papers about, totally oblivious to the greeting.

"Uh, Mr. Mole?" said Roger. "Uh, you look very busy, but, uh, can we talk to you for just a minute?"

The mole remained unaffected by the threesome and continued to smoke, read, mutter and shuffle papers about. His enlarged, front feet and broad claws moved quickly and continuously in a whirlwind of activities.

CHAPTER 11: MR. MOLE

Arthur approached the desk, peered way, way up and tried to get the
mole's attention. "Good evening, Mr. Mole! You look very fine this
evening, sir. What are you doing?"

Again, the mole didn't answer and continued to smoke, read, mutter
and shuffle papers about. The gray color of his thick fur looked entirely
washed out against the bright, red wall behind him.

The trio looked at each other and shrugged. "Do you think we're in
the right place?" asked Arthur.

"Uh, I don't know," replied Roger. "He doesn't seem to have any ears.
Maybe he can't hear us."

"Look!" exclaimed Poopsie. "He's writing something down."

They shuffled closer, inch-by-inch.

The mole remained preoccupied as he made notes, with a pencil
twice the size of himself, on a huge sheet of paper that trailed behind
him.

The threesome moved even closer.

"Uh, Mr. Mole?" said Roger again, a bit more loudly this time. "Mr.
Mole?"

Finally, the mole peered down with a horrible scowl on his face. "Yes?
Well? What is it? Can't you see I'm busy?"

Arthur took another step forward. "Hello, Mr. Mole. Would you have
time to talk to us for just one minute?"

"No," he shouted. "Can't you see I'm busy? Go away!" He

CHAPTER 11: MR. MOLE

immediately continued to write notes, holding the huge pencil in his broad claws.

Poopsie marched past Roger and Arthur. "Excuse me?" he said in a very loud voice. "Excuse me!" he shouted.

The mole glared over the rims of his thick lenses and then continued to do what he was doing.

"This is important, mole!"

The mole looked at Poopsie for a moment, took off his glasses and sat back in his gigantic mole chair. "Really? Well, how more important is it than Einstein's theory of relativity or any of his other theories about time and space? Can it be more important that that? Well?" he demanded in quick phrases.

Poopsie did not know what to say because he had never heard about Einstein or his theories. So he shrugged and said, "I really don't know, mole."

"Then be off with you. All of you." He dismissed them with a wave of his large hand.

Roger took a few steps forward. "Uh, Mr. Mole? This is really, really important, uh, in the big scheme of things, if you know what I mean."

The mole stared at Roger through glassy, hooded eyes that were barely visible. "In the big scheme of things, you say? Hmmm...is that so? Then tell me, bulldog, what is it then?"

Little Arthur found his way to the front. "Mr. Mole, we are trying to find Mr. Moon. Can you help us, sir?"

CHAPTER 11: MR. MOLE

The mole let out a long sigh through his long, flat snout. "Is that what this is all about? Finding Mr. Moon?"

"Uh, yes, sir."

"Well, don't you see? Don't you see? It is all very relative. Very relative."

The threesome had absolutely no idea what the mole was talking about. "Can you explain what you mean?" asked Arthur.

"You see," the mole continued in an authoritative manner, "Einstein was a very smart man. Very smart, indeed. He stated that matter and energy are interchangeable. Matter is nothing but a form of light. And light is nothing but form of energy. Ergo, matter and energy are basically the same thing. Do you know what I mean? Do you?"

"Uh, with all due respect, Mr. Mole, we don't," said Roger in his low, low voice.

The mole spoke very quickly until he was practically out of breath. "Let me explain it to you in another way. According to all my calculations, everything you perceive with your eyes has been created by the energy of your thoughts and feelings. Oh, this is deep, very deep. Do you know what I mean now? Do you?"

Arthur replied with trepidation, "Well, sir, we kind of understand. Sort of, I guess. A toad tried to explain the same thing to us a while ago."

"A toad, you say? A toad? How very interesting. How very interesting, indeed."

"Listen, mole head, excuse me for interrupting your dissertation, but we are trying to find Mr. Moon. If we don't find Mr. Moon before

CHAPTER 11: MR. MOLE

Mr. Sun's shift ends, we will never see in the dark again. We are up against a wall, mole, because time is running out."

"Uh, can you help us, please?" pleaded Roger Earl of Henry.

The mole shrugged. "Mr. Moon, you say? Yes! Yes! Yes, I can help you! All you have to do is continue down the path to your next signpost. That's all you have to do. Down the path...yes...that's all you have to do. Now be off with you. All of you!" The mole buried his head again in his books and papers and notepads.

"But, Mr. Mole? There's a huge, brick wall behind you! How can we continue down the path?" asked Arthur.

The mole gave his dense, velvety fur a scratch, turned around and looked at the trio again. "A brick wall, you say? A brick wall? I don't see a brick wall. I don't."

Poopsie became agitated. "Look, mole face, our time is running out. We have to find Mr. Moon soon. Tell us how to deal with this huge wall!"

The mole put his glasses back on again, which enlarged his eyes to huge proportions. "I told you. I do not know what you are talking about. I do not see a brick wall. If you see it, that's your problem, not mine."

Poopsie, Roger and Arthur stood silent for a few minutes and tried to gather their thoughts. "Uh, why do we see it and you don't?" asked Roger. "That's, uh, weird."

"Not weird at all, bulldog. Not at all," the mole replied quickly and assertively. "You see, whatever you hold in your thoughts will manifest in the outside world. After all, like I said before, thoughts are just energy. Yes, they are. Just energy, I say. And energy manifests into matter. Therefore, you must always, always expect a positive outcome. If you don't, the negativity of your thoughts will create roadblocks. You have a brick wall in your thoughts, you see, and I do not. Ha-ha on you...you have actually sabotaged yourselves. Yessiree! It is quite remarkable how you did that. Create a brick wall, that is. But you must realize that the wall is only an illusion. It is just a reflection of your thoughts. Everything is just an illusion, you see. Ergo, by bringing this truth from your unconscious mind to your conscious mind, the wall should dissolve. It's just that simple."

"That is not particularly clear to me, mole breath," Poopsie sneered. "How do we get through the wall?"

The mole looked at Poopsie impatiently. "Have you not been listening to a word I have said? The brick wall does not exist. It is only an illusion. You have created it yourself through your negativity. In order to dissolve it, you must realize that it is only an illusion. It's just that simple. You see, the thing is, you will never find Mr. Moon unless you think positively and productively or you will continue to create roadblocks. You will continue to sabotage yourselves."

And then the mole disengaged himself entirely from the discussion by continuing to do whatever it was that he was doing.

So Poopsie, Roger and Arthur huddled together once again to decide upon their next plan of action.

"I think we should close our eyes and walk right through it, like we did at the stream," said Poopsie.

"I don't agree," replied Arthur. "The mole said the wall was just an illusion. If we concentrate on walking through it, then it still exists, right?"

"Uh, I don't get it," said Roger, who was baffled beyond his comfort level. "It all seems pretty creepy, if you ask me."

CHAPTER 11: MR. MOLE

"Didn't you hear what the mole said, dog brain? He said the wall was just an illusion. He doesn't see it, right? So that must mean that we have created it with our thoughts. Maybe it's there because we expected a roadblock."

"No, YOU expected a roadblock, Poopsie," corrected Arthur. "You were the one who said we were up against a brick wall."

"That may be, mouse head. But how do we remove the roadblock?"

"Didn't Mr. Mole say that our awareness should be enough to dissolve the wall? The awareness that it is just an illusion? That we created it ourselves? That it's not real? That's what Mr. Mole said."

"We just dismiss it, right?" asked Poopsie as he straightened his glasses. "By realizing that we caused it ourselves."

"Uh, so it's not really real?" asked Roger.

"The mole doesn't even see it," said Arthur.

"I sabotaged all of us with my thoughts," confirmed Poopsie.

Suddenly, their senses perceived a change. The wall was no longer red. It was a light pink. Its edges were fuzzy and irregular as though it were moving or transforming into another shape. In just a minute or two, it appeared to slowly evaporate right before their eyes.

"Oh, wow!" exclaimed Arthur. "It's gone!"

"Uh, that's unbelievable," said Roger Earl of Henry. "Really unbelievable."

Poopsie continued to stare into the empty space behind the mole. "Wow! It's really gone!"

CHAPTER 11: MR. MOLE

The mole eyeballed the trio and muttered quickly, "You must expect a good outcome at all times, no matter what the circumstances. In other words, in order to find Mr. Moon, you must have faith. That is the law, and I have spoken. Now go away."

He then lit up another giant cigarette and began to smoke and to read and to mutter and to shuffle papers about.

CHAPTER 12

MRS. BULLDOG

With the determined looks of soldiers on their faces, they quickly proceeded down the path.

"Come here, Arthur," beckoned Roger. "I know you are the leader, but if you sit on my head we will all move a lot faster. Besides, I don't want to, uh, step on you."

"Thanks, Roger," replied Arthur as he scampered up Roger's hind leg, across his back and up to the top of his head.

"Hey, look, air heads," pointed Poopsie. "Way, way down there. I see something. Do you see it?"

They all stopped for a moment and squinted.

"Yes! There is something down there, all right," said Arthur, "but I can't see what it is."

CHAPTER 12: MRS. BULLDOG

"Uh, well, then let's keep going," said Roger in his low, low voice. "We'll find out when we get there."

As they got closer, Roger could see the outline of what appeared to be another animal. "Looks like it could be a large, uh, raccoon."

Arthur hid under Roger's red and white checkered tam and peeked out to snatch a glimpse. "I don't see any rings around its eyes."

"Nope. I don't think it's a raccoon," said Poopsie. "Besides, we all have to think positive thoughts, remember? No more roadblocks."

"Let's, uh, move a bit closer then," suggested Roger Earl of Henry.

So the trio slowly approached the mysterious creature until they were within closer visual range.

"Huh? Does that, uh, look like a bulldog to you?"

Poopsie half closed his eyes and craned his neck. "Yep. It's a bulldog all right. What do you think it's doing out here?"

The bulldog sat fearlessly and steadily in the middle of the path with no sign of hostility in her brown, velvety eyes. Her head was large and broad with a wide muzzle. Reserved and dignified, she wore a beautiful rhinestone collar around her neck and a striking pink bow on top of her head. Even in the dimming light of the day, her fur looked sleek and lustrous.

"It's a girl dog," Arthur whispered in Roger's ear. "And her fur is the same color as yours!"

Roger stood still, just staring at the lovely bulldog. He had never seen a more beautiful bulldog in his life.

CHAPTER 12: MRS. BULLDOG

"Uh, hello, Mrs. Bulldog," he said taking off his hat and forgetting that Arthur was still in it. "Very nice to meet you."

The bulldog smiled. "Thank you, Roger Earl of Henry," she answered in her soft voice. "How are you?"

He shrugged. "Well, uh, it's kind of been a rotten day, ma'am."

She laughed, displaying her pearly, white teeth. "Then perhaps you should rest for a while. You all looked pretty tired."

Roger kept staring at her, rendered speechless by her beauty. He could not figure out why he was so drawn to this bulldog. She was lovely, but there was something else…something he could not quite put his finger on. Her voice and countenance were so soothing. She made him feel warm and fuzzy inside. Without speaking, he moved closer.

Poopsie noticed Roger's odd behavior and marched up to Mrs. Bulldog. "Ma'am, with all due respect, we are in a bit of a hurry. You see, we are trying to find Mr. Moon before the lights go out. Can you help us out, ma'am?"

Her chocolate brown eyes twinkled. "I can try," she replied sweetly.

Arthur jumped out of Roger's hat, scurried to Mrs. Bulldog and stood between her front paws. "Oh, Mrs. Bulldog, you are so beautiful. May I touch your fur?"

"Oh certainly, Arthur the Mouse. I'd be honored."

So Arthur slowly rubbed his little mouse hand up and down the bulldog's front leg. "Oh, wow," he exclaimed. "It feels just like velvet and you smell so good!"

CHAPTER 12: MRS. BULLDOG

She lowered her eyes demurely. "Thank you, Arthur."

Meanwhile, Roger continued to inch his way closer to the bulldog. His nose glistened with moisture as he sniffed high into the air. Slowly and surely he shuffled nearer and nearer.

The revelation came like a thief in the night. In just a few seconds, and with no warning at all, every cell in Roger's big, old body stood at attention as the identity of the mysterious bulldog was swiftly resolved. His legs buckled underneath him as he breathed in the truth through his large, black nostrils.

He rolled his head towards the sky and let out a mournful howl. "Hoooooowl! Hoooooowl!"

Thinking Roger was having a full-blown heart attack, Poopsie ran to his rescue. "Are you okay, Roger? You look pretty awful. Are you okay?"

But Roger just kept howling. "Hoooooowl! Hoooooowl!"

Arthur the Mouse ran to him. "Roger, Roger, Roger! What's wrong? What's wrong? What's wrong with your legs? Why are you making those sounds?"

Roger's paws rolled into fists and his back tensed as he glared at Mrs. Bulldog. Emotion cursed through his tired body like sheets of lightning as his heart pumped furiously in his chest.

Then finally, his body folded into a heap like a rag doll. "Mommy," he said in a very small voice.

She sat down beside her beloved son and tenderly brushed his forehead with her paw. "Hello, my little one."

CHAPTER 12: MRS. BULLDOG

Roger's body heaved and trembled as the tears flowed. "It is really you, isn't it?"

"It is, my son."

Roger's grievous sobs echoed deep into the forest, as his heart broke wide open.

"Why, Mommy? Why? Why did you do it? Why did you give me away? What did I do wrong?" he wailed. "Was it because I was just an ugly bulldog?"

Mrs. Bulldog wiped the tears from Roger's face and looked deeply into his eyes. "You did nothing wrong, Roger. And look at you! You are the most handsome bulldog I have ever seen!"

He pulled away. "Then why did you leave me? Why did you leave me all alone?"

"Oh, my goodness! I did not leave you! I lost you! Your papa and I and your five brothers and sisters were playing by the river that fateful day. You were such a playful little thing. You slipped and fell into the river and the current swept you far, far away. I've been looking for you ever since, my dear, sweet Roger." She began to weep softly. "I've missed you so very much."

"That's probably how you ended up at the castle, Roger," said Poopsie quietly.

Arthur whispered into Roger's ear, "And that's why you are so afraid of water."

As Roger put his arms around his mother and wept, all the horrible thoughts and feelings he had of being abandoned, all the anger, all the

CHAPTER 12: MRS. BULLDOG

hurt, and all the sorrow vanished into her warm, loving body.

"Oh, Mommy, I've thought about you every single day."

Poopsie and Arthur hugged each other and cried openly as they watched their friend melt into his mother's body.

Time stood still as years of hurt dissipated into the dark, cool air.

As Roger embraced his mother, he noticed something else down the path that looked rather remarkable. As though they were posing for a family portrait, more bulldogs stood like statues in the middle of the path, all in a row, all holding hands, all different from the next, and all staring straight ahead with unblinking eyes at Roger. One bulldog appeared to be taller than the rest and was crying.

Poopsie did not notice that Roger was preoccupied with a new situation. "Roger, we really have to go now. We will see your mother again soon."

"Roger," he called again.

Roger disregarded Poopsie and said quietly to his mother, "Are those my brothers and sisters, Mommy?"

She smiled and looked at him with profound love and affection. "They are, son. They, too, have missed you so much."

"And the tall one?"

"Papa."

When Roger saw the love and acceptance in the eyes of his entire family, he unabashedly wept with joy. Although he had been wishing for this

CHAPTER 12: MRS. BULLDOG

day for a very long time, he knew that if it weren't for Merle the Squirrel and his pail of nuts, this moment would not have come to pass.

For an instant, he wondered if this magical forest had somehow, in its own mysterious way, helped him achieve his most heartfelt dream in the direst of circumstances. He pondered on whether Mr. Moon had actually led him to his greatest triumph amid his deepest adversity.

"Mommy," he said, "my heart is bursting with happiness. We have so much to look forward to...all of us. Right now, Mommy, we have to find Mr. Moon. Merle the Squirrel's life depends on it. Can you help us?"

"Don't forget about Freddie, too," added Arthur.

Mrs. Bulldog turned to Arthur and Poopsie and took their hands in hers. "Thank you for befriending my Roger. He's a good bulldog and he means well. I know now that he has a good home and good friends. I know he is loved. Thank you so very much."

She turned to Roger. "Son, with forgiveness in your heart, you can find Mr. Moon. That is the law and I have spoken. Go to the next signpost around the corner. Go quickly. We will see each other again soon."

Full of tears and totally spent, the threesome left.

Roger appeared to have a renewed skip to his gait as he thought about all the days ahead that he would spend with his family. For the first time in his life, he felt important and special and worthy and regal, as a bulldog should.

And unbeknownst to Roger Earl of Henry, or anyone else for that matter, yet another great change in his life had taken place on this memorable day. He had lost his speech impediment and would never, ever stutter again.

CHAPTER 13: MR. LEOPARD

CHAPTER 13

MR. LEOPARD

Poopsie raised his grimy paw to hold his friends back. "Sshhh! There's something in that tree over there. I can smell it."

"I can't see anything," said Arthur.

"Sshhh! No, I'm sure of it."

"What does it smell like?" whispered Roger.

Poopsie stood as still as a statue and mouthed the words, "I can hear it now. I can hear it breathing. And it sounds really big."

The threesome huddled together for comfort.

"If it's really big, it could eat us," fretted Arthur.

"Yah," whispered Poopsie. "What should we do?"

CHAPTER 13: MR. LEOPARD

"We could run," said Roger.

"No!" Poopsie replied. "Too big. It would outrun us."

"Should we hide?" asked Arthur in his scared, little mouse voice.

Poopsie squeezed his eyes into slits. "There!" he pointed. "I see something. It's in the tree. I saw it move!"

They huddled even closer.

"Should we run now?" cried Arthur in a panic.

"Sshhh!" said Poopsie. "Let me think. Let me concentrate."

Silent and trembling, the trio kept their eyes on the tree, which pointed forty feet into the darkening sky.

"Look, up there!" Arthur pointed to the upper branches of the tree. "The tree is moving!"

"The tree isn't moving, mouse brain. Something IN the tree is moving!" said Poopsie as he craned his neck. "Wait! Why is that rope dangling from the top branch of the tree?"

Upon saying that, a shadowy, mysterious figure slinked from one side of the tree to the other, with its graceful, meter long tail following behind.

"Mary, Mother of Jesus!" exclaimed Poopsie. "The thing hanging from the tree is its tail. And it's huge!"

"Oh, man," said Roger. "The tail looks six feet long."

Roger, Poopsie and Arthur squeezed up closer as they kept their eyes riveted on the enigmatic creature that moved slowly and silently.

"Look!" hollered Arthur who was much too afraid to whisper. "What's that?"

Two, grayish green eyes pierced the imminent nightfall.

"Oh, man," moaned Roger. "Oh, man."

Suddenly, they heard a growling, hissing, spitting noise and the huge creature leaped with remarkable strength and agility from the highest branch of the tree and landed squarely in front of them on all fours.

The salivating cat hungrily licked its lips and walked a wide circle around them. He let out a deep roar and his white canines pierced the dusk.

"What's the matter?" he jeered at the threesome who had frozen on the spot. "Never seen a leopard before?" He grunted and hissed and continued to stalk the trio with his magnificent claws spread wide.

Hyperventilating in his fear, Arthur struggled to find his voice. "Oh, please, Mr. Leopard. Please don't hurt us!"

Roger's voice wavered in a higher pitch than usual. "Mr. Leopard, leave us alone, sir. We don't mean you any harm. We are just three travelers who are looking for Mr. Moon."

Poopsie hissed and spat at the leopard, but felt himself feeling faint from his fright.

The elusive leopard seemed to disappear, then reappear. His reddish brown coat with dark spots camouflaged him well against the backdrop of the forest.

CHAPTER 13: MR. LEOPARD

"I can leap from the highest tree and land silently on my feet," he sneered. "I can jump ten feet into the air and catch my prey like a thief in the night," he mocked. "I can run like a gazelle without struggling for my breath," he teased. "I can hang upside down from a tree branch and surprise even the mightiest beast of the forest," he taunted. He glared at the threesome through sinister eyes and hissed, "You don't have a chance against me. I am the Big Bad Wolf of the forest, the most feared creature of all."

"Oh, please, Mr. Leopard!" screamed Arthur. "Oh, please leave us alone!"

"We must get by you, leopard," murmured Poopsie who had collapsed into a vulnerable sitting position. "We have to find Mr. Moon before Mr. Sun ends his shift or we won't be able to see in the dark! And look! Mr. Sun is almost gone!" he said, pointing to the west with a weary paw.

The leopard looked down at them and laughed. "You have to find Mr. Moon? That's an admirable mission. But you can't run away from your fear now, can you?" he said haughtily. "It won't let you."

The leopard swelled in size to the height of the treetops and blocked out the remaining light. He let out a mighty roar, which shook the ground they stood upon and made the largest tree trunks sway back and forth like bulrushes in the wind.

Poopsie's hungry, worn out body trembled so hard that he held his paw tightly over his heart for fear it would fall out of his chest. As he could no longer support his body weight, he crouched at the mercy of the leopard.

"Oh, leopard, please have mercy on us," he begged. "We are defenseless and weak. There cannot be enough meat left on our bones to satisfy your hunger."

CHAPTER 13: MR. LEOPARD

Swishing his long tail at the height of the treetops, the leopard sneered and grunted. "Don't you see what you have done?"

Arthur the Mouse, who was dwarfed under the leopard's white belly, retreated into a little ball and whimpered.

Roger mustered the courage to look at the hungry leopard. "Please have pity on us, Mr. Leopard. We mean you no harm."

The leopard's eyes shone like dazzling jewels. "Don't you see what you have done?" he asked again. "Whatever you dwell on will expand. The more afraid you get, the bigger I will become. You cannot run away from your fear. You must dismiss it immediately or you will die. I will eat you."

Poopsie's terror paralyzed him. Somehow, he gathered enough strength to speak. "You go away, leopard," he demanded in a raspy whisper.

The leopard lowered his head, cocked it to one side and meowed like a kitten in Poopsie's face. "Well, well, pussycat. Haven't you learned a thing in your journey thus far? Did you not learn from the toad that your reality is determined by your beliefs? You chose to walk across the stream rather than drown in it by merely changing your beliefs, didn't you? Did you not learn from the mole that your negativity would create brick walls? You chose to dissolve the obstacle rather than be blocked by it, didn't you? Have you not already learned that whatever it is you dwell upon will eventually show up in your journey? Am I not a projection of your fears? Rather than continue to create these illusions, when will you finally tame your thoughts and feelings and expect only a positive outcome?"

The leopard began to grow in size again. "See, I will only get bigger. You must conquer your fear to get rid of me or your journey ends right here."

CHAPTER 13: MR. LEOPARD

"Yes, yes," Poopsie finally muttered in a peculiar moment of clarity.

"What is it, Poopsie? Hurry! What is it?" screamed Arthur.

"Don't you see?" he replied quickly. "Don't you see what we have done? We have sabotaged ourselves again! Didn't we express our fear when it started to get dark in the forest? Or if we didn't express it, didn't we feel it?"

"I felt really scared," admitted Roger.

"Me, too. And guess what? Our fear manifested into this gigantic beast of a leopard. The only way we will rid ourselves of him is by not being afraid. Didn't Mr. Moon say we were only as big as our faith? Didn't he? How can we be afraid if we have faith?"

Poopsie panted with exhaustion as he slowly crawled on his belly to Arthur and Roger. Then, with his eyes fixed on the creature, he shouted, "You go away, leopard! I am taking charge of my friends now and I am no longer afraid of you! Do you hear me? I am not afraid anymore! We will find Mr. Moon, and Merle the Squirrel, and Freddie the Mouse. Nothing will stop us! We will fulfill our mission no matter what! Go away, leopard! We are not afraid of you anymore! You will not stand in our way!"

Upon hearing those words, the leopard began to shrink until he finally became as small as Arthur the Mouse.

Arthur's eyes widened like black cherries. "Oh, Mr. Leopard, you're shrinking, you're shrinking!"

Poopsie, who was too debilitated to move, glanced at the tiny leopard and then collapsed on his side.

CHAPTER 13: MR. LEOPARD

"I am not shrinking," said the leopard to Arthur. "It is your fear that is shrinking."

"Oh, gosh," exclaimed Arthur. "You can't hurt us anymore. You are disappearing!"

Roger walked up to the tiny leopard and peered down. "We are running out of time, Mr. Leopard. Can you please help us find Mr. Moon?"

As the leopard continued to diminish, he answered, "You must be fearless to find Mr. Moon. That is the law and I have spoken."

On that note, he vanished completely.

"He's gone! He's gone!" screamed Arthur the Mouse.

"Hurry," yelled Roger.

Poopsie had fallen unconscious in the cold, wet grass, unbeknownst to his two friends who had already run ahead.

CHAPTER 14

MR. COTTONTAIL RABBIT

"Hey!" shouted the small rabbit in a loud, shrill voice.

Unaware of the rabbit's beckoning call, Roger continued to run full barrel down the path with Arthur bobbing up and down under his red and white checkered tam.

The rabbit thumped his large, hind feet on the ground and screamed even louder, "HEY!"

"Stop!" Arthur cried out to Roger. "Did you hear that? What's that thumping noise?"

Roger came to a screeching halt, perked up his ears and looked around. "I don't know, Arthur. But where's Poopsie?"

"OVER HERE!" yelled the rabbit again.

"Look," pointed Arthur. "It's a cottontail rabbit. He's trying to get our attention!"

CHAPTER 14: MR. COTTONTAIL RABBIT

Arthur and Roger ran over to the brown speckled creature with big eyes, big ears and a tufted, white tail that resembled a cotton ball.

"Oh, dear," the blue-eyed rabbit lamented as he looked at an enormous, red pocket watch hanging from a chain around his neck.

"What is it, Mr. Cottontail?" asked Arthur.

"Behind you! Look behind you! Hurry!"

They turned around and saw something lying across the path. "Could that be Poopsie?" fretted Arthur.

The trio ran back to the lifeless form. "It is Poopsie!" cried Arthur. "Wake up! Wake up!"

Roger kneeled down on his stubby knees. "Poopsie, are you okay?" he asked frantically.

"Of course he's not okay. Look at him!" said the cottontail.

Poopsie appeared to be quietly resting on his side as though he were sleeping, but his glazed, empty eyes told a completely different story. His tongue protruded from the side of his partially opened mouth like a sodden, blue petal.

"The poor cat, after all," added the rabbit. "He had the living daylights scared out of him by the leopard. And he hasn't had anything to eat or drink since early this morning at the stream. What do you expect?"

"Wake up, Poopsie. Please wake up," implored Roger.

Arthur tried to rouse him by patting him on his face. "Is he dead, Mr. Cottontail? Is he dead?" Arthur sobbed.

CHAPTER 14: MR. COTTONTAIL RABBIT

"Almost," replied the rabbit as he looked at his pocket watch again.

"What should we do? What should we do?" shrieked Arthur. "He can't die!"

"Indeed," calmly replied the cottontail. "But if you stay behind to help him, you may not find Mr. Moon before Mr. Sun leaves. If that is the case, you will never again see in the dark and more importantly, you will never find Merle the Squirrel or Freddie the Mouse."

"What about our friend, Poopsie?" ranted Arthur hysterically. "Is his life not as important as Merle the Squirrel's or Freddie's?"

"Indeed it is, but as you can see, he's in no shape to join you," answered the rabbit.

"No!" screamed Arthur. "That's not fair! That's not fair! We can't leave him behind!"

Roger grabbed Poopsie by the shoulders and gently lifted his head. "He's breathing, but just barely. Oh, please, Mr. Cottontail. We have to find Merle the Squirrel and Freddie, but we're not willing to do it without Poopsie. So, please, please tell us what to do."

"Hurry!" sobbed Arthur as he rubbed Poopsie's arms and legs.

The cottontail rabbit checked his pocket watch again and then looked intensely at both of them. "Very well. Since you are so persistent, there's a mud hole up ahead just around the next corner. Why don't you look there for some food and water? If you are fast enough, perhaps you will be able to revive your friend and still find Mr. Moon. However, I must tell you that your time is quickly running out."

Roger tried to think at lightning speed. "Arthur, you can run much faster than me, so you go and try to find some water. Here, take my hat and use it to carry the water back. I'll stay with Poopsie."

In a panic, Arthur took Roger's hat and ran as fast as he could towards the mud hole.

"I found it! I found it!" he screamed. "And I see a pond here, too. I'll have to walk through the mud to get to the water!"

"Be careful, Arthur," Roger yelled back. "You don't know how deep the mud is."

"I'll walk across the mud hole just like Poopsie walked across the stream. I know I can do it!"

So little Arthur did a very amazing thing. All alone and afraid for his friend's life, he closed his eyes, imagined a hard, dirt path across the mud hole and began to run to the other side.

Halfway across the mud hole, he suddenly stopped.

"Hurry," cried Roger. "Don't stop, Arthur, or you'll sink."

"But there's something under my foot!" Arthur reached down into the mud and ran his hand over the object he was standing on. It felt like a marble. By searching the area around him, he soon discovered that quite a few of these smooth thingamabobs were buried in the same vicinity. He reached further into the wet mud with his little mouse hand and grabbed hold of one of them. Holding it close to his eyes, he peered at it for a moment before he suddenly realized what it was. "It's a nut! It's a nut!" he squealed. "Look, Roger! I found a nut! And there's lots more!"

Carefully carrying a single nut in Roger's red and white checked hat,

CHAPTER 14: MR. COTTONTAIL RABBIT

Arthur ran to Poopsie and placed the filbert beside his head. "I'll go get the rest!"

With absolutely no problem whatsoever, Arthur the Mouse ran across the mud hole fifteen times in total without falling through and managed to carry each of the fourteen nuts back to his friend, Poopsie, as well as a hat full of water.

Before long, and upon smelling the delectable nuts, Poopsie's whiskers began to twitch, his lifeless tongue turned rosy pink and his eyes slowly became alert and focused.

"What happened?" he asked groggily.

Roger and Arthur joyfully hugged him. "You fainted from hunger and exhaustion, Poopsie. We thought you were dead," said Roger. "But Mr. Cottontail helped us. He showed us where to find food and water and we still have some time left before Mr. Sun's shift ends."

Poopsie stared back at them through dazed eyes. "Where did you find the nuts?"

"Over there," Arthur pointed. "In the mud hole by the path!"

"That's really something, isn't it?" said Roger. "I wonder how the nuts got there."

After a brief moment of silence, Poopsie stood up, brushed himself off and looked at Roger and Arthur. "I'll tell you how they got there, poop heads. Merle the Squirrel buried them there. That's why his pails were never full. He buried half the nuts so he would have some left over for the winter."

Roger and Arthur looked at him blankly. It took a minute for Poopsie's statement to sink in.

CHAPTER 14: MR. COTTONTAIL RABBIT

"So you mean he didn't eat them after all?" asked Roger. "You mean he was hiding them for us all along?"

Poopsie nodded thoughtfully and the trio stood staring at one another.

"Oh, gosh," said Arthur. "Oh, gosh."

"Why didn't he tell us?" asked Roger.

"Why?" replied Poopsie. "Because he knew we wouldn't care. We didn't need the nuts, after all. We all live in a castle, for Petie's sakes. We're probably the only friends he has and gathering the nuts ensured he would see us once a week."

"Why did he have to bury them?" asked Roger. "Why didn't he just keep collecting them as usual?"

"Because, you double poop head, nuts don't grow in the winter. Get it?"

"Oh, boy," said Roger quietly.

"We don't deserve to be his friends," whispered Arthur. "Why would he want us as friends, anyway, after the way we treated him?"

Poopsie riveted his eyes on the ground. "He accepted our faults and forgave us, that's why."

The rabbit observed the threesome as they came to terms with a newly found truth. "You are correct, Poopscapaleon," he said. "That stupid, annoying, useless squirrel, through the generosity of his heart, risked his life in order to feed all of you throughout the wintertime. While the three of you took shelter in a castle on a hilltop, Merle the Squirrel battled the elements. Do you know how many times he almost lost his life to a predator? Do you know how many times he cried himself

CHAPTER 14: MR. COTTONTAIL RABBIT

to sleep? Do you know how many times he almost froze to death in the dead of the night? And because there are no coincidences, I might add, on this particular, fateful day, the very nuts that he stashed in the mud for further purposes saved your life, Mr. Appotamus."

Poopsie, Roger and Arthur hung their heads in shame.

The cottontail rabbit finally broke their silence. "Judging another creature of the forest is a very grievous act. It is the greatest act of violation you could bestow upon another individual. By judging another, you breed gossip and you break hearts. Judging another creature is telling them that, in no uncertain terms, your life is more important than theirs. Although Merle the Squirrel always knew you made fun of him, he still loved you. You were his only family, after all. Do you understand what I'm saying?"

Poopsie slowly lifted his head. "Yes," he said quietly. "We do."

"You must go now because time is running out," said the cottontail rabbit as he checked his enormous pocket watch once again. "Keep following the path. You will find Mr. Moon by loving others, rather than by judging them. That is the law and I have spoken."

And so off they went, emotionally spent and physically exhausted, their hearts bursting with their newly found love for Merle the Squirrel and their footsteps faltering with painful remorse for their actions.

CHAPTER 15

MR. SNOWY OWL

With reverence, Roger painstakingly carried his filthy hat containing Merle the Squirrel's nuts. He walked stiffly with his head held high and his arms outstretched as though he were offering a freshly slaughtered lamb to the ancient gods. Determined not to lose any of the ten nuts, he kept his body steady by taking deep breaths and holding them for as long as possible.

Poopsie, who had become sullen and introspective, followed Roger like an obedient shadow. Arthur trailed a few feet behind Poopsie and struggled to keep up.

In about fifteen minutes, they came to an intersection. The path they were on split into two paths, one veering sharply to the left and one veering sharply to the right.

"That's weird," said Arthur. "We haven't seen anything like this before."

"Which way should we go?" asked Roger, who was haggard and worn and a few pounds lighter around the belly.

CHAPTER 15: MR. SNOWY OWL

Dumbfounded by their new dilemma, Poopsie took his glasses off and rubbed his sore eyes. "To be honest, I really don't know."

Arthur scampered up Roger's back and sat on his head to get a better view. "We're running out of time! We're running out of time!" He pointed to Mr. Sun who was now a glowing, red ball on the horizon.

Feeling utterly defeated at this juncture, the trio sat down and huddled together for warmth in the middle of the intersection. The mood was very somber, indeed.

Roger cautiously placed his red and white checkered tam on the cool ground without spilling any filberts. They all peered down at the hat as though it were a treasure chest filled with gold.

"Would you like another nut, Poopsie?" asked Roger politely.

"No, thanks, Roger. Why don't you and Arthur have some? You must be really hungry."

They both just shook their heads.

Poopsie stared at Arthur, who was now so weak and so frightening thin that his skin looked transparent over his fragile mouse bones. Exchanging a troubled look with Roger, he reached over and took Arthur's tiny hand in his. "Are you doing all right, mouse head?"

Arthur began to cry. "I miss Freddie. And I feel so bad about Merle the Squirrel. And you gave us a real scare back there, you know? It's all been so hard," he sniffled and snorted.

"Listen to me, Arthur. Roger and I are so very proud of you. You've traveled a long distance in the past few days, and for a little guy like you, you've shown a lot of strength and courage. You ran across a

CHAPTER 15: MR. SNOWY OWL

mud hole, all by yourself, to save my life and you never thought once about leaving me behind. And you continue to be brave as we press on to find Merle and Freddie. You're a very special mouse, Arthur. I'm sure Merle the Squirrel wouldn't mind if you had just one of his nuts."

"But I can't, Poopsie. They don't belong to me."

"Very well, Arthur. Then why don't you ride in my pocket the rest of the way? Do you want to do that, little man?"

Half his normal weight and weakened by starvation, Arthur's shoulder bones looked like toothpicks as he slowly climbed up Poopsie's arm and slid into the small pocket of his red and white flowered smoking jacket.

Roger wiped a tear from his eye, but said nothing.

"So which way do you figure we should go, Roger?" asked Poopsie. "Should we go left or should we go right?"

"I can't think anymore, Poopsie. My brain hurts."

"Well, we have to make a decision soon, Roger, or our time will run out."

Arthur poked his little head out from inside Poopsie's pocket. "What if we make a mistake? What if we go the wrong way? Then we'll never find Merle the Squirrel or Freddie."

"We've come this far and we're not going to fail now. Let's start by having some faith that we're going to make the right decision, okay? After all, the toad proved to us that our reality is determined by our beliefs. So let's only keep positive thoughts in our minds. We don't

CHAPTER 15: MR. SNOWY OWL

want any more roadblocks, do we? And we must be fearless! Merle the Squirrel and Freddie's lives depend on us. We don't need any more leopards bearing down on us."

"So which way do you want to go, Poopsie?" asked Roger.

Poopsie closed his eyes and sighed. "I wish I knew, Roger. I wish I knew."

Suddenly, they heard a loud swoosh!

"Hoot, Hoot!" greeted the pure white owl that landed on a nearby tree branch. His round, yellow eyes peeked through disks of stiff, white feathers and remained fixed as he swiveled his head from right to left and from left to right. "Hoot, hoot! Hoot, hoot!"

The owl spread his wings for a stretch as his curved, black claws gripped the tree branch. "Good evening, my friends. I've been expecting you!" He flew silently to a higher tree branch, where his stark, white coloration contrasted the darkening sky.

Arthur buried his head in Poopsie's pocket. "Don't let him see me," he whispered quickly. "He could be hungry."

"Don't worry, Arthur," answered Poopsie as he gently patted his little friend's head. "I won't let anything happen to you. I promise."

He walked to the tree and looked up at the owl. "Mr. Snowy Owl, can you help us, please? We have had a very long day and our time is running out quickly. We have to find Mr. Moon before Mr. Sun ends his shift. Otherwise, we will not be able to see in the dark. And if we cannot see in the dark, we won't be able to find our friends, Merle the Squirrel and Freddie the Mouse. If we cannot find our friends, they may not survive the night. The three of us are all very hungry and tired and desperate. We have very little strength left. Can you help us out?"

"We have been fools, Mr. Snowy Owl," added Roger. "We have treated Merle the Squirrel horribly and we are suitably ashamed of ourselves. If anything happens to him, or to Freddie, we will never, ever forgive ourselves."

"Hoot, hoot!" replied the snowy owl through his coal, black bill. "What do you have to say about this, Arthur the Mouse?"

Arthur's head popped out of Poopsie's pocket like a jack-in-a-box. "How did you know I was hiding in here?"

"I have very acute hearing, my little friend. And there are no secrets in the forest. Don't be afraid. I won't harm you."

Arthur looked at the owl through his sunken eyes. "Mr. Snowy Owl, please help us find Mr. Moon. Please help us, sir."

The bird took flight, landed on a tree stump and looked down at them through his powerful, binocular eyes. His head pivoted every which way as he searched the area for dangers. "Can you tell me what you have learned on your journey thus far?"

"We have learned that our thoughts are very powerful," said Arthur the Mouse. "We walked across a stream by changing our thinking."

"We have learned about humility," added Poopsie. "Especially me."

"And love and compassion," said Roger in his low, low voice.

"And we have learned that we can create our own roadblocks as well as undo them," said Arthur.

CHAPTER 15: MR. SNOWY OWL

"And we've learned to be fearless," said Poopsie.

"And to see good in everything," added Roger.

"And to understand there are no coincidences," said Arthur.

"And not to judge," said Poopsie very quietly. "Our lives will never be the same, Mr. Snowy Owl," he added.

The owl's intelligent eyes looked like disks of fire as he continued to appraise them. "To find Mr. Moon, my friends, you must find your genius. By finding your genius, you will always be assured of staying on the right path. When you find your genius, you will ask the right questions. When you ask the right questions, the right answers will come. That is your genius!"

"How does that work exactly, Mr. Snowy Owl?" asked Roger.

"My good bulldog, suffice it to say, the great forest is always here to support you. So just ask the right question and the right answer will come."

The owl lifted his wings and flew into the darkening sky. "Good-bye! Good-bye! Good luck! Remember, to find Mr. Moon, you must find your genius! That is the law and I have spoken."

"What are we going to do now?" asked Arthur the Mouse whose cold, dehydrated skin looked paper-thin.

"Sshhh!" whispered Poopsie. "I'm thinking. We're so close!"

Poopsie continued to think about all the things he had learned over the course of the day. He felt he could trust what the wise, old owl had said. He believed that if he asked the right question, the right answer

CHAPTER 15: MR. SNOWY OWL

would come. He wasn't sure where the answer would come from, but he had already resigned himself to the fact that some things could not be explained in a short time span and should only be accepted.

"Let's just ask the question, then. Let's just ask which way we should go."

So the threesome held hands in a circle and asked the question out loud. "Should we go left or should we go right?"

They continued to repeat the question over and over again as Mr. Sun began to make his final exit. The sky continued to dim and the air drew a renewed chill.

Arthur pointed to the sky. "Look! Look!" he shouted. "Mr. Sun is going! He's going!"

Poopsie raised his paws to the sky in a final, desperate attempt to get an answer. "Mr. Sun! Mr. Sun! Should we go right or should we go left?"

"Bye-bye!" answered Mr. Sun.

"No! No! Don't go!" screamed Arthur through his sobs.

"I'll be seeing you," replied Mr. Sun.

Roger stood motionless as he beseeched Mr. Sun. "Please, sir, please help us. We must find Merle the Squirrel and Freddie."

"Wait a minute!" said Arthur. "Mr. Snowy Owl said we had to ask the right question to get the right answer. Maybe we're not asking the right question."

"Of course!" said Poopsie, slapping his forehead. So with a slight twist to his question, he turned to Mr. Sun one last time. "Which way should we go to find Mr. Moon?"

"It's time for my rest now! Goodnight everybody!" answered Mr. Sun. "Good-bye!"

As Mr. Sun waved, a single sunbeam from his hand cast its final light upon the left path.

"Look," shouted Arthur as he pointed to the ray of illumination. "Over there! We have to go that way!"

"Hurry!" yelled Poopsie.

So with eight clues behind them, they ran down the left path with just a quick glance over their shoulders to see Mr. Sun dip behind the horizon. The ten remaining nuts bounced and rattled, as Roger gripped his red and white checkered cap tightly between his teeth.

CHAPTER 16
THE TRUTH

Poopsie and Roger felt their chests tighten and their leg muscles burn as they began to climb a gradual, but daunting hill.

"Mary, Mother of Jesus! It's worse than Mt. Everest, for Petie's sakes! We're never going to make it to our next signpost on time!"

"Keep running, Poopsie. Just keep running," huffed and puffed Roger who ran as fast as his weary, stubby legs could carry him. "We have to stay positive. Watch what you say and just keep running."

"You're right, my friend, we're almost there. We have to have faith! Maybe there's something over the crest of the hill," pointed Poopsie, who tried to keep one eye on the path and one eye on Mr. Sun.

Then quietly, and without any fuss, the night blackened as Mr. Sun's radiance completely disappeared beyond the horizon.

"I can't see anymore!" screamed Arthur the Mouse. "I'm blind again!"

CHAPTER 16: THE TRUTH

"Be brave, Arthur! We only have one more signpost to go!" shouted Poopsie.

Like gentle, mothering hands, the magical branches of great, majestic trees guided Roger and Poopsie through the darkness as they continued to race up the hill. Arthur, in sheer terror, tumbled about in the pocket of Poopsie's tattered, red and white flowered smoking jacket.

Emotionally exhausted from desperation and physically weakened from hunger, they pushed their limits to reach the summit. Then, like in that brief instant on a rollercoaster, when one just barely crests the top of a very steep hill and can see nothing ahead but open sky, when the fear of the unknown can incapacitate even the bravest soul, they looked inside themselves for all the courage they could muster to sprint down the other side of the hill, in the dark, as fast as they could.

However, upon reaching the summit, they screeched to an unexpected halt. To their utter amazement, a new world unfolded before them like a beautifully painted, colorful canvas.

They stood in awe as they peered down at the most breathtaking sight they had ever seen.

With eyes fixed and mouths agape, they stared at a brightly illuminated, vast, perfectly circular valley in a kaleidoscope of vibrant colors. The endless, green forest surrounded the glen like a fortress and a cloudless sky of resplendent, periwinkle blue filled every other nook and cranny with exquisite vividness.

Mr. Sun hung high above with a grin on his face as the magnificent light of his radiance saturated the valley. There was no darkness in this part of the forest. Everything here reflected his light and bathed in his warmth.

CHAPTER 16: THE TRUTH

Not only was this awe-inspiring, new world suffused with intense colors, it was also inundated with the laughter and chatter of all the entities who dwelled in it. All the signpost creatures, from the roaring leopard to the teeny spider, frolicked with one another with no fear or hostility. A sense of peace pervaded the air like a warm, summer breeze.

"Hey, look!" cried Arthur the Mouse. "There's Mr. Mole!"

They could hear the funny looking, earless mole muttering and shuffling and fussing about, as he blew smoke rings high into the sky. "Hello! Hello!" he yelled out as he looked over his thick glasses.

"There's Miss Dandelion," remarked Roger Earl of Henry.

The dandelion stood erect and greeted the trio. "Hello, friends," she said. "It's so good to see you!"

In the distance, Mr. Cottontail Rabbit snoozed with Mr. Toad on a rock near a clear, blue pond. One of the rabbit's ears gently rested on Mr. Toad's eyes and shaded them from the sun.

They could hear Mrs. Robin and her babies giggling with glee as they played tag with Mr. Snowy Owl in the open sky.

"Look!" pointed Poopsie. "Way up there!"

They all looked at the tallest tree in the forest, an old, oak tree, which towered well above all the other trees at the north end of the valley. Cutting the circular landscape in half, their path led right up to the base of the oak tree's gigantic, ringed trunk like a royal, crimson carpet leading to a throne. They could tell, without any shadow of a doubt, that this tree was a very important tree, indeed. At its very most tip sat a majestic eagle on watch, its brilliant eyes afire and alert.

CHAPTER 16: THE TRUTH

"It's Eddie the Eagle! It's Eddie the Eagle!"

The trio ran down the hill with renewed strength and hope. The meadows were full of red, blue, green and yellow flowers that swayed in the breeze every which way, casting their lovely scents in every direction. The threesome felt so intoxicated by the sweetness in the air, they could barely contain themselves.

"Wow! Wow! Wow!" squealed Arthur in sheer delight as he tumbled and rolled in the lush green grass.

Poopsie looked around at the unfamiliar landscape. "We must be in heaven!" he exclaimed. Then he scampered through the flowers, right and left, left and right, feeling the softness of their delicate petals.

Roger, who was completely dumbfounded, just sat on his rather large bulldog rump and peered around with a foolish grin on his face. "Well, dog gone it," was all he said.

"Come on! Come on! I bet we'll find our last signpost in the tree," urged Poopsie.

So the very tired, very hungry, but very ecstatic creatures ran down the homestretch of the pathway, which led to the base of the large, old oak tree. Upon reaching the tree, they found they were dwarfed by its immensity. Looking up as high as they could, they shielded their eyes from Mr. Sun. The oak tree was so tall that it seemed to pierce the heavens with its regal spire.

"Is anybody there? Is anybody there?" they yelled simultaneously. "Are you there, Mr. Moon?"

Mr. Moon's elusive voice gently caressed the rich, dense forest. "In order to find me, you must seek the truth! Keep going!"

CHAPTER 16: THE TRUTH

So Poopsie mustered as much strength as he could and climbed a quarter of the way up the tree trunk. Looking through the lush, green leaves of the long branches, he called out, "Is anybody there? Is anybody there?"

Merle the Squirrel woke up Freddie the Mouse who was curled up into a little ball beside him. "Freddie! Freddie! Look! Look! It's Poopsie! They are all here! Poopsie, Roger and Arthur!"

The two friends scampered to the end of the tree branch and hollered in the loudest voices they could muster, "We're here! We're here! We're up here!"

The trio harkened to the little voices. "Is that you, Merle the Squirrel? Is that really you?" cried Poopsie.

"Yes! We're up here!"

Poopsie climbed down the tree and joined Arthur and Roger. They all stood back to search the top of the big, old oak tree. They finally spotted Merle the Squirrel and Freddie the Mouse clinging to a branch way up high.

They shrieked. They danced. They screamed. "Freddie! Freddie! Merle! Merle!"

The scene was pandemonium as the threesome threw kisses to Merle and Freddie, while shouting words of thankfulness, of kindness and of affection.

"Are you okay, Merle and Freddie?" shouted Poopsie.

"We're fine, Poopsie," replied Freddie in the biggest mouse voice he could find. "Eddie the Eagle has been looking after us."

CHAPTER 16: THE TRUTH

"Merle the Squirrel," he shouted again, "It's important that we find Mr. Moon. He told us that we must seek the truth. Can you tell us where he is?"

Merle took a few more steps forward on the sturdy tree branch that supported him and stood in plain view of his friends. "Yes," he replied excitedly. "I can help you! I can help you! I can tell you where Mr. Moon is!"

"Please tell us, Merle the Squirrel. We have been looking for him for a very long time. Where is he? Where is Mr. Moon?" Roger asked. "We have to tell him that we've found you. We have to thank him. And we want to know the truth."

Merle took a deep breath, stood on his hind legs and pumped up his little squirrel chest as full as he could. He smiled so widely that the rest of his little squirrel face seemed to almost disappear. "I'll tell you where Mr. Moon is!"

"Where is he?" urged Arthur.

Pointing to the center of his chest, Merle screamed at the top of his little squirrel lungs, "He's here! Mr. Moon is here! He's right in here!"

"He's in you?" asked a somewhat baffled Poopsie whose eyes opened a bit wider.

"He's in all of us!"

"You mean inside?" asked a perplexed Roger.

"Yes!"

"You mean he was with us all along?" cried Arthur.

CHAPTER 16: THE TRUTH

"Yes!" screamed Merle again. "He's never left you! Don't you see? He's never left you! He never, ever will! You don't have to go anywhere to find him. All you have to do is look inside. That's where he is and that's where he will always be." He pointed once again to his little squirrel chest. "He's right in here!"

"Well, what is the truth then, Merle?" insisted Poopsie.

Merle the Squirrel's smile radiated like a beam of sunshine. "The truth, Poopsie, is the part of you that never changes. It's the part of you that will always be connected to Mr. Moon." He spread out his arms to embrace the forest and everything in it. "This truth is in all of us! We are all connected to Mr. Moon and we are all connected to each other. Don't you see?" He threw his little squirrel hands to his cheeks. "Anything is possible!"

All five creatures remained quiet for a long minute. To all the other entities in the valley, it seemed that time had momentarily stood still as they awaited the great revelation to sink into the deep recesses of the creatures' hearts. No other truth could be more important. No other truth could be more life-altering.

"Oh, Merle!" exclaimed Arthur. "We have so much to think about!"

"Well, dog gone it, anyway," added Roger in his low, low voice.

Poopsie took a few steps forward and looked straight up. "Hey, Merle! We found your stash of nuts in the mud. Are you hungry? Do you want some? We saved them for you!"

"And I saved some for you, too!" he cried as he pushed the gigantic pail of nuts from the top branch of the old oak tree. The pail fell to the ground and the nuts scattered everywhere.

"Oh, boy," said Roger. "We have a lot of nuts now."

CHAPTER 16: THE TRUTH

Poopsie's eyes filled with tears and he joyfully punched his fists into the air. "Merle! You are some kind of squirrel! Would you like to come live with us in the castle?"

The little squirrel's hands flew up to his mouth in utter joy. "Do you really mean that, Poopsie? Do you?"

"Yes, Merle," added Roger Earl of Henry. "Why don't you come and live with us. There's lots of room. We can all go out nut hunting together. As a team."

"You can be the leader," said Poopsie.

"We can share stories about what we have learned in the past few days," said Arthur. "And every night, you can tell us stories about Mr. Moon."

Overwhelmed by the invitation, Merle the Squirrel burst into tears. "Yes! Yes! I want to live with you! I want to be with you all the time!"

So Merle ran down the big, old trunk of the oak tree, with Freddie hanging onto his neck for dear life, and jumped into the arms of Poopsie.

"Oh, for Petie's sakes!" exclaimed Poopsie as he hugged them both. "I don't think I've ever been happier in my entire life!"

At that precise moment, the brightness of this perfect world started to fade from color to black and white as the sky began to darken.

"Look!" pointed Freddie. "Look, up there!"

As the five creatures turned and looked upward, they saw a most remarkable thing. Mr. Sun was slowly disappearing as a giant, lunar globe slipped in front of him.

CHAPTER 16: THE TRUTH

"It's Mr. Moon!" proclaimed Merle the Squirrel as they watched the full, round, white splendor finally block out the sun's entirety. Mr. Moon became as black as coal except for the glory of a brilliant, orange ring, which adorned him like a crown.

"They've become one," said Arthur excitedly.

"Behold!" commanded Eddie the Eagle from his highest post. "Behold!"

The new world held its breath throughout the breathtaking solar eclipse. A moment of silence filled the valley as all the entities bowed reverently before this miraculous sight.

Then gradually, very gradually, Mr. Sun and Mr. Moon once again went their separate ways.

Or did they?

'Let's go home' were the first words spoken as the five creatures turned around and started their long journey back to the castle. They left all the nuts behind because food and rest were not important to them at this point. For some reason, they knew they would find everything they needed on their way home. Nor did they walk in single file. Rather, they walked five abreast, heads held high, hands held tightly, conquering the path with each deliberate step.

But it was the big, old oak tree that got the last word in before the saga of this journey ended.

"So it is," he said. "When you get to be as old as me, you understand

CHAPTER 16: THE TRUTH

that the most remarkable part of your journey begins when you realize that the light shines from within you, not from without.

"It is this light, at the core of your being, that illuminates the forest. And it is this very light that will enable you to grow tall and mighty like me.

"So declare you magnificence! Be thankful for who you are and more will be given to you!

"And remember, we are all united on this journey. Each creature you meet along the way is a signpost whose purpose is to give clues to guide you closer to Mr. Moon.

"Love yourselves and love others unconditionally.

"Create beauty and abundance through faith and expectation.

"Replace doubt and fear with trust and wisdom.

"Reach high with your thoughts because they become the foundation of your reality.

"Ask the right questions and the right answers will come.

"Do not judge anyone or anything. Everyone and everything in your life is meant to serve you in some way.

"Use the wisdom of the universe for support and guidance by paying attention to the synchronicity in your life.

"Acknowledge that you are wholly responsible for your circumstances and have the power to change them at any time.

CHAPTER 16: THE TRUTH

"Find the power by keeping good things in your heart and your mind at all times.

"Go now, creatures! Go now and share your light! Share your knowledge with all who care to listen.

"Until we meet again, may the power of manifestation, vested in you by the universal Law of Attraction, bring health, wealth and happiness to all the days of your lives.

"All is well!"

ABOUT THE AUTHOR

W.K. ATKINSON

After a successful corporate career, Wendy went on to receive honors in Journalism and pursue her writing. She is now committed to helping people of all ages, cultures and backgrounds achieve their highest goals in every aspect of their lives. Founder of Mr. Moon & Friends, Wendy now teaches motivational seminars on the Law of Attraction, offers personal coaching and continues to write. For more information visit W.K. Atkinson's website at http://LawOfAttractionToday.com.

LaVergne, TN USA
03 February 2010
171867LV00004B/5/P